TALKING WITH DOG

A
NOVEL
BY
MARK ROPER

For my wife Dee and my daughter Katie.
True survivors.

If the past cannot teach the present and the father cannot teach the son, then history need not have bothered to go on, and the world has wasted a great deal of time.
Russel Hoban, The Lion of Boaz-Jachim and Jachin-Boaz

The truth is that our race survived ignorance; it is our scientific genius that will do us in.
Stephen Vizinczey, Truth and Lies in Literature

The end of the human race will be that it will eventually die of civilization.
R.W.Emerson

CHAPTER ONE

The year and the date you must choose.

On the Western slopes where the grass remains green and primroses grow, a lonely worker bee scavenges for pollen. It is ten minutes past nine in the morning.

Turning your head to the East you can see a distant city poking its concrete fingers towards a heavily, polluted sky. It was once a polite horizon. It was once a clear sky. The name and description of this city must be named by you for the sake of familiarity. Remember it well for it will be for the final time.

The sound we suddenly hear is not of thunder. The sound we hear that rudely snaps the silence over the Western slope is of galloping horses. There are four horses in total. Three greys and a black, their hides already tainted with sweat and a white, salty froth.

The lonely working bee does not have the time to move. It is quickly killed beneath the heavy hoof of a horse. It is left crushed in the soil.

The four riders on the horses all wear the same uniform: dark blue riding hats anointed with the familiar Border Patrol insignia, flak jackets over pale green shirts, brown leather boots and jodhpurs tailored of denim. On their belts, secreted accordingly, each man carries a holstered Glock pistol, a set of handcuffs, a walkie -talkie and a slim mobile phone. Every man wears a pair of identical sunglasses.

Bent forward over the saddle, the riders have pointed their horses' flaring nostrils toward the very distant shape of a canyon. The plateau between them and their destination is flat, interrupted by sage brush and tortoise shaped, sun kissed rocks. A soft heat wave undulates.

Two minutes have passed since the death of the working bee.

CHAPTER TWO

The canyon is some two hundred yards in depth, its walls towering on either side some forty feet high. Its floor is crammed with boulders and narrow dusty pathways. A few saplings cling to the shadows. A horned lizard bathes in the day's heat, wary of hunting kestrel.

A vulture rides a thermal, circling the canyon. His wings held aloft, he looks down on the canyon below. His is the only movement.

A silver painted sedan car is parked at the mouth of the canyon. Its panels are dusty and dented and its two front tires are punctured. The driver's door hangs open. Two empty cardboard boxes litter the ground. A fly with a swollen belly hovers over what is a splatter of blood on the upholstery of the driver's seat.

A man is seated on a boulder shaped like an acorn at the rear of the canyon. From this pedestal he has a good view of the canyon as well as the approaching, distant, horsemen. The man is dressed in a grey suit that is torn at the elbows. Somehow, the man has lost a shoe. Dry, encrusted blood shows on the chest of his pale cream shirt.

The man is in his mid to late forties and slightly balding. He is unshaven. His name is David Erasmus. On the rock, near his feet, rests a small, metallic box the size of a cigarette case. A green light blinks from the case and below the green light is a red, rubber tipped button. Set neatly beside this box is the familiar shape of a Swiss army knife.

David squints in the sun. His eyes are tired and redness shows. He wipes at his brow with his sleeve and swats at a hovering, curious fly. He can see the riders. A plume of dust trails them. David sniffs, his nasal canals wet with the fluid of recent tears.

David picks up the Swiss army knife and he selects the main blade. From his jacket pocket he withdraws a fob watch. The timepiece is old, inherited from his father who was awarded it by a select group of engineers upon his retirement. The watch is so designed that when looking at the time, one can see into the working mechanisms of the piece. Perfectly balanced brass cogs, ratchets and pinions turn against each other, every turn adding (or subtracting?) a new second to David's life. David turns the watch over in his hand. Using the blade of the knife, he begins to scratch into the silver plated hull.

Just before David turned the fob watch over, he checked the time. It read twenty minutes after the hour of nine.

CHAPTER THREE

The four horses have settled into a canter and the riders sit back lazily in their saddles as if in armchairs. There are sounds of garbled voices being transmitted over their walkie- talkies. The words being broadcast are inconsistent. "...is airborne." "Do you copy?" "...nine o five is onto a visual" So the chatter continues as the horses' hooves add dust to a windless air.

It is at this moment that a rider spots the flash of light to the rear of the canyon: a brilliant flicker of sunlight bouncing off metal.

The rider does not rein his horse in. "That has to be him," he announces. "There, at eleven o' clock."

"You want me to call it in?" The rider that asks is the youngest of the four. His sunglasses mirror his youthful eyes.

"Yes. Do it. The man is a murderer."

The young rider earnestly reaches for his walkie-talkie as his heels dig into the flanks of his horse.

David puts aside the fob watch. He rests it on the rock as he checks the approaching horsemen. He is aware that they have seen him. It was he that ensured sunlight would ricochet off metal. David digs into his shirt pocket. His fingers are trembling as he removes the match thin tube of blue print. It is less than an inch in length. He holds it between two fingers and gently places it under the weight of the fob watch.

The time is now twenty-five minutes after nine.

The vulture continues flying his lazy circle. His head shifts. He blinks against the breeze.

Satisfied that the tube of blue print is secure from uninvited breeze, David again picks up the Swiss army knife. The instrument offers childhood memories but these must remain forgotten now as David wipes the blade on his sleeve. (To character and even at this moment of his life, he is cautious of his own hygiene). David opens his mouth. He brings the blade up and into his mouth. The heat of his breath mists the blade. With his free hand, David pulls back his upper lip into a snarl. He closes his eyes against the sweat that is freely running down his forehead. He bares the lateral incisor to his fingers, to the blade of the Swiss army knife. The flesh on his knuckles has paled.

The first jab of the blade at the base of the incisor causes David to wretch. He spits away the sour bile that has risen in his mouth as he struggles to inhale through his nostrils. A tear forms in the corner of his right eye and it collects dust as it descends. David lifts his upper lip. A thin line of blood stains his gum. He brings up the blade yet again and allows it to hover there as he opens his eyes and looks out across the canyon floor. He focuses on the approaching horses. He thinks only of the approaching horses.

With a deft jab and a twist, David thrusts the blade deep and up into his gum toward the root of his upper, left incisor. He will have to cut at least a third of an inch deep.

The time is twenty-eight minutes past nine.

On the Western slopes, where the bee lays dead and some five miles from the canyon, the three camouflaged vehicles appear in convoy. Above them, its rotors whistling a steady tune, a dark blue helicopter follows. There are flashes of faceless men behind tinted windows. The Border Patrol insignia is again prevalent. Once on the flatness of the plateau, their bonnets pointed toward the canyon, the vehicles are soon lost in their own cloud of dust.

The riders draw up their horses to the left of the canyon's mouth. They dismount and tether the horses to an obedient thorn tree. Steam rises off the animals' flanks. The riders remove their Glock pistols. The young rider cocks his weapon.

"There's no need for that."

"Why? You said yourself he's a murderer."

A rider holds up his cellular phone. A CCV captured image of a harassed David Erasmus about to enter a silver sedan is on display. "I checked his profile. He's un-armed."

"But that was yesterday."

"Computer is never wrong."

They approach the abandoned car and a rider quickly looks into the vehicle. Another flips an empty cardboard box, whilst the remaining two riders scan the depth of the canyon. A film of fine dust now smothers their sunglasses.

The lead rider calls out. "David Erasmus?" His voice has a dull, bored echo to it in the canyon. A horse snorts to their left. "There are four of us down here and we are armed. Do you understand?"

David's mouth is bloody. He has removed the incisor. The pain he is in is reflected in his eyes. Droplets of blood have saturated the lapel of his shirt, blossoming like ink on blotting paper.

David's response is impeded by the blood in his mouth. "Yes. Yes I understand." A pink tipped bloody bubble hangs on his chin. David keeps his attention on the four riders as he grasps the roll of blue print between trembling, dusty fingertips.

"Then you know why we are here?" The rider who asks the question moves quickly to his right and deeper into the mouth of the canyon. His intention is to get a better view of David. His riding boots kick up a little dust.

If this rider was to have looked down at his boots at that moment, he would have spotted the small, wax wrapped package attached to the underside of the rock. But he does not as his focus is on David. The wrapping and its contents are of military origin. It is known as C4.

David's eyes are a soup of tears and sweat as he forces the thin roll of blue print into the cavity once occupied by his lateral incisor. He struggles against the need to wretch as his fingers make contact with his thickened tongue. With his thumb, he applies pressure to the blue print, forcing it up and into his gum. His small scream is drowned in the back of his throat.

"I asked you, if you know why we are here?" The rider's voice is suddenly intrusive, its echo sounding like a kettle drum in David's ears.

With his fingers still in his mouth, David unconsciously nods. He senses dizziness. The blue print is in place, buried in his gum. Like an exhausted marathon runner, David sits down and puts his head between his knees. His chest heaves. He can smell urine. The black sock on his shoeless foot is soaked in his own piss.

"Yes. Yes I heard you." David's words are at sea. He tries to regain strength. "Yes. And yes, I know why you are here." This time he hears his own voice bounce off the canyon's walls. It reassures him; proves he exists.

"What time is it?"

David's question confuses the riders. They glance at one another questioningly.

"He wants to know the time?"

A rider shrugs. "No harm in telling him."

The younger rider checks his military issued watch. "It is after nine thirty. "

David spits blood. "I mean the precise time. Please."

"It is precisely nine thirty-eight," the young rider replies in a patronizing tone.

David checks his fob watch. The instrument reflects the identical time as the rider's. David pulls out the winding arbor by one movement. The sound of the click is pronounced in the silence; almost like a twig snapping underfoot.

A horse neighs and its ears lay back. A little white shows in the animal's eyes.

David's fingers poise over the winding arbor. He steadies his breath.

There's a quick cackle of static filled voices over the riders' walkie-talkies; a burst of confused gibberish. A rider tweaks a button, silences the gibberish.

The rider who stands deepest in the canyon calls out. "We are here to arrest you on suspicion of the murder of Nathanial Trader. We are told you are in possession of a document that belonged to Mister Trader - do you have it?"

David sweeps his look over the canyon walls, then back down to the riders. "The document does not belong to him. It never did. But yes - yes, I have it."

His voice rings flat, almost retiring, as if being asked a question he has answered many times before.

"Then we are coming up to you, Mister Erasmus."

"Of course you must. Come up here, I mean."

A rider looks behind him, toward the plateau. The approaching cloud of dust tells him the support posse is closing in. The sun glances off the windshields of the military vehicles and the helicopter sits over them like a hovering bird of prey.

"Should we wait for them?"

"No. He's harmless. Split up and I'll take point."

David begins to turn the winding arbor. He advances the minute hand by two minutes. He doesn't reset the arbor, he doesn't SET the time. He simply waits with his fingers on the brass, ridged appendage. The watch now reads forty minutes past nine.

The riders are walking forward using the tapered dusty trails between the boulders; a pair of boots narrowly passes yet another package of C4 that is tucked in a crevasse. An active spider web hangs nearby; a decaying carcass of a moth swings forlornly from its silky veins.

David touches his mouth. The blood has stopped flowing but his lips feel bulbous and aflame. He leans forward over his knees as he watches the approaching vehicles in the distance. Their shapes are becoming recognizable now as they spear through the curtain of heat wave. David reaches for the metallic box, keeps it in his left hand, the fob watch in his right.

"I think it's about time now," David suddenly calls out. He remains squatting on the boulder, chin on his knees, rocking in suffering on his haunches. His throat is tight and dry.

The leading rider pauses. He lifts his hand, gesturing for his team to stop. "What did you say, Mister Erasmus?"

"What's he got in his hand?"

"I can't see. Can you?"

"Negative."

"Put it down, Mister Erasmus!"

David closes his eyes. The action squeezes tears; they run freely, trailing recent stale salty paths. He squeezes his ears closed, shutting out the echoing voices of the riders.

"Put it down now!"

David sets the watch into movement. The seconds hand sweeps across the face. He has advanced time by two minutes.

The Vulture, keeping its altitude, glides smoothly over the canyon. There's a whisper of sound as he adjusts his flight path, feathers against glass.

The horses react as if stung by hornets or bees. The grey, a mare, rears, snapping her reins, her rump slamming into the horse beside her. A black stamps its feet impatiently, tossing its head left and right, nostrils suddenly flaring and showing a purple panic. Two horses break free from their tether. They turn toward the plateau, loose stirrups slapping against saddle leather. The grey follows, her mane wild as she tosses her snorting head.

"The horses - what's with the horses!?"

"Put it down, Erasmus!"

Fingers search and grasp for the winding arbor. His vision blurred by pain and panic, David now re-sets the time on the fob watch. He retards the time by sixty seconds, allowing the minute hand to sweep backwards across the ornate face. The winding stem feels pathetically small in his fingers.

The lone horse stands shivering on the spot, its flanks pulsating. Its head is dropped toward the ground as if committing to a race already lost.

Nine thirty nine. Time is retarded by one minute. Sixty seconds of lived in time, stored, archived amongst cogs, ratchets, pinions and arbors. Preserved and locked away in a fob watch.

The Glock pistol has a standard magazine of seventeen rounds.

The down thrust of the helicopter's blades adds a petticoat of dust around the travelling vehicles. The effect is almost embryonic. Shock absorbers soak in the unbalanced terrain as reinforced tires turn rapidly.

"Put. It. Down."

"IT IS ONLY TIME!" This is David's voice; it is guttural; disembodied.

David's eyes suddenly open like a man a rudely awakened. A slight moment to focus, then a calmness, an inner peace, washes over his eyes. David turns his head to the left and looks into the empty space beside him. He smiles. He smiles at a-nothing; emptiness.

It is the smile a father offers his son after a term of absence.

The Glock's firing mechanism has a spring-loaded firing pin that is cocked in two stages. When the pistol is charged, the firing pin is in the half-cock position.

Nine forty.

"Hello, Joseph." David tells the empty space on his left with a slight, nervous smile. "I'm glad you came." David's voice is rasping.

The Glock's 9mm round slams into David's right shoulder. His body twists spasmodically as the bullet enters muscle and flesh and exits cleanly. He rights himself. A half open smile of aloofness hangs off his bloody lips. His right arm now lame, David barely manages to hold the fob watch.

He remains focused on the vacant space. He frowns as if being asked a question. "Of course it's me, Joseph," he responds a little impatiently.

The rider, who fired the shot, settles after the recoil. He senses members of his team drop defensively to the ground either side of him. He digs his boots deeper into the soft, grainy sand. A high pitched electric squeal shouts over his walkie-talkie, its origin or language unknown. A new cartridge slips into the chamber.

"What's he saying? He's saying something?"

"Put. It. Down. Now."

David Erasmus holds the fob watch in his right hand. In his left hand he grasps the metallic box, its green eye blinking. He sits on his haunches, leaning forward, his head, though on his knees, turned toward an empty space on is left. His injured shoulder is at an obscure angle. In defiance, a slow drop of blood oozes from his gum onto his lower lip. He can feel the urine wetness of his sock.

"Joseph - you must make it right," David tells the space. "The answer is in my mouth. I love you."

Faceless shapes of men in a vehicle with an amber blue dragon flying overhead.

A youthful rider lying prone with dust on his sunglasses and eyes filled with alarm.

Wax wrapped CT4 explosive beside a riding boot, the pencil shaped detonator visible.

David brings up the metallic box.

The Glock fires: The whistle of its second bullet cleaves the hot and humid air.

David presses the red-tipped rubber button on the metallic box.

My name is Dog.

I am a simple creature: I eat from a simple carcass. I ask for no more or less. I am good.

I fly your sky. From a height I witnessed the beginning of the end.

In my simplicity I do not profess to know your sciences, your mathematics, your nucleus, atoms and fission.

From aloft, riding a thermal, I experience the detonation.

My wings are buffeted by the shock waves that precede the wrath.

My body is pummelled.

I close my eyes to the whiteness of the light before I begin to spiral away.

Toward what and where, I do not know.

Only time will tell.

A time left recorded in an inscribed fob watch.

On your wide-screen television set, there is an image of an over brilliant sun. Then your television shuts down.

On your iPod there is an image of a mountainous section of an iceberg collapsing. Then your iPod goes blank.

On your mobile phone, whatever the make, there is an image of a wind generator. It crumbles like an autumn leaf underfoot. Then your mobile phone goes blank.

On your computer screen there is an image of dead cattle on a ravaged land. Then your computer shuts down.

Through your window you see the dust as it advances like a Tsunami. Then you can see no further.

CHAPTER FOUR

The once grassy plains have changed. All hint of greenery has gone. It is hot, dry and a lazy devil-wind spirals lethargically in the West.

The skyline of the city you named earlier has disappeared. Not even a shadow remains. Those people that survived have moved on to distant places.

The cause of The Event is simple. It requires no scientific explanation. Mother Nature has always walked with small steps, learning and progressing during her gradual journey through time. We humans have ignored that learning. We have outpaced our own, what should have been, measured strides. We have started running before we have truly learnt to walk.

Mother Nature has simply put the brakes on. She has shortened your stride. She has retarded life in the hope that we will learn to walk again.

The solar storm, you remember, lasted for eight months; in some areas, longer. The crust of the planet was left flecked like the hide of a spotted hyena; flecked with disaster zones, places where the few survivors, mainly the young, managed to migrate from. Some were fortunate, others not so.

On the same horizon line we begin to see an approaching vehicle, swimming in the heat-waves. The vehicle is a truck--a beast, twin exhausts looming over the high driver's cabin. Such is the metallic gleam -- pearl silver -- the vehicle has a ghostly, spiritual quality about it. It keeps approaching. There is very little engine noise; like a soft whistle of air through parted lips.

The sun is now a white, hostile orb; iris burning.

Welcome to the town that your God, Law, Time, Nature and society has forgotten. A line of bungalows now stand brick deep in ever increasing mounds of shifting sand, their structures built from salvaged remains of brick, wood, plastic and metal. A shanty town that whispers of a past you may remember, but shouts of a sad present.

An army of salvaged wind-pumps turn angrily in the wind, their battle now to suck water from an unyielding soil. Three crippled wind generators turn in the stale air, probably creating enough power to light a bulb or two.

A hint of ill repaired solar panels can be seen perched on the crudely constructed roof tops.

A small Church offers its imperfect steeple to a cloudless sky. There is one shop, a general dealer. There are no cars, no gas pumps nor signs of children. The sight of a blossoming flower is rare. There is a monotonous twirling of dust and the ricocheting of bright sunlight off metal.

At the far end of the only street, outside a house, a group of people have gathered. There is also a cart and a donkey.

Inside the house, in a narrow bedroom, Reverend Dickinson, spectacled, stands looking out the window. He's holding a Bible. Reverend Dickinson is stooped under God's forgetfulness. It is a heavy burden for him and the slope of his narrow shoulders demonstrates that.

Suddenly there is a woman's scream from within the room and it scares the crap out of Reverend Dickinson. He spins on his heels.

"Well?" Reverend Dickenson asks the midwife that is bent over the prone body of the woman who is about to give birth.

The woman giving birth again screams. She is over the age of seventy and her wrinkled, sunburnt flesh contorts grotesquely. Rivulets of perspiration gather in the valley of her wrinkles.

The midwife, who is in her late sixties, glances quickly toward Reverend Dickinson. "It's coming. Help me."

"No!" The Reverend almost shouts his response.

The pregnant woman mumbles incoherently.

"I need light. Move away from the window."

The Reverend Dickinson does, his glasses shining like mirrors in the heat. Through the small window, he can see the group of people gathered outside in the street. An elderly woman sits on a wooden stool. She is knitting a garment. It is pink and suited for a newborn child. The knitting needles click furiously in her hands.

The midwife works, her heavy face sweating profusely.

A bowl of bloody water is dipped into and out of.

"Please God," whispers Reverend Dickinson, still hypnotised by the rhythm of the knitting needles.

"Come on, Mary, come on...you have to push, Mary! I can see the head!"

There is another scream and the tension shows in the Reverend's shoulders. He wants to turn and look, but he cannot.

The midwife suddenly shouts. Her own breathing is heavy. "It's out! It's a..."

Reverend Dickinson spins on his heels. "It's a what? Tell me."

Reverend Dickinson makes eye contact with the midwife as he struggles not to look at the bloody mess that he knows the midwife must be holding.

The midwife holds the Reverend's enquiring look momentarily, then she vomits.

Reverend Dickinson gulps in air and closes his eyes. He inhales and exhales and he tries to compose himself. He straightens his back, finding strength from somewhere.

"Wrap the...wrap it up," he finally says with an edge of hostility.

Then he leaves the narrow room, the Bible clutched to his chest.

Out on the arid plain, a small swarm of locusts fly through the dry air, the sound of their wings like crackling flames. The swarm is flying directly toward the approaching vehicle whose pearly sheen mirrors the flaccid desert shrub.

On the rear of the truck, in a makeshift wire mesh cage, there is a collection of materials: canvas tents, a battered electric oven, spades and an assortment of crowbars. The carcasses of recently killed hares hang from a butcher's hook close to the rear window.

The driver of the truck is Joe. He is in his early twenties. His skin is tanned. His attention is on the track ahead and the approaching swarm of locusts. The manner, in which Joe drives, his posture, hints that he is at peace out here in the new nothingness. He is a man in control of his personal journey. The pair of hands that grip the steering wheel are strong, their palms lined with callous.

Joe, to use an expression commonly used in the rapidly growing language of The Event, has come from 'Out There.'

The swarm of locusts approach. The texture of the insects' wings flare in the sun.

Joe studiously watches the swarm. There is no malice in his eyes, only a soft, intriguing smile on his lips. A song played by Deep Purple whispers from the reconstructed cassette player. Joe's knuckles tighten on the steering wheel.

Abruptly, there is a sound in the truck's cabin: it is a 'hiss' like air escaping from a large inner tube. The noise is repeated, followed by shuffling - akin to shaking out a duvet - and then a muted 'squawk'.

Joe doesn't shift his focus from the approaching swarm. "Not now, Dog. Not now," he whispers.

The swarm of locusts is directly in line with the front of the moving vehicle. A collision is imminent.

The hissing and the shuffling sound again intrude into the cabin.

"I said not now, Dog!" Joe's voice cracks like a whip.

The swarm of locusts is about to meet a windscreen. Only a few feet separate them.

But the insects do not pulverise themselves into the glass. As if parted by a miraculous force the swarm divides and flutters harmlessly either side of the vehicle's huge bonnet, noisily passing by the passenger windows.

Joe exhales and his hands relax on the steering wheel. He shifts slightly in the driver's seat, gathering himself like a man who has exited a tunnel. Then he turns and glares across to the passenger seat.

"Next time you do that, it's the cage for you. Understand."

Sitting on a makeshift perch on the passenger seat, is a vulture. The bird views Joe with fixed, hooded eyes as it shuffles its feathers.

"I was sharing the road, Dog -- never interrupt a man when he is sharing the road and trying to avoid a collision. It's important to avoid a collision, Dog. That's how people get hurt." Joe leans over, turns up the music. "Trust me. I know what I'm talking about. Ends up with wreckage everywhere and it's hard to pick up the pieces - hard to even FIND the pieces after a collision."

Dog shifts on his makeshift perch and returns to staring at the dirt track ahead.

I am Dog. We have already met, as I flew over the canyon, some twenty years ago. I am a friend, in spirit, with the man Joe as he seeks out a similar carcass as I, but not for the same reason, as Time will tell.

CHAPTER FIVE

Reverend Dickinson steps from the house onto the sandy surfaced porch. He carries the deceased infant wrapped in white linen. Behind him, in the doorway, the midwife fights away her tears. The Reverend looks at the waiting group of people.

The people look at Reverend Dickinson. Every person there, male and female, are over the age of sixty. Their clothing has faded of colour as much as life has faded in their eyes and posture.

An elderly man, Mister Richards, stands to the rear of the meagre crowd. Beside him is a rustic hand - cart loaded with an antique chair, a painting, a suitcase and a soft child's toy.

Some of the older women remain seated, their knitting now dormant on their laps, knitting needles held loosely in their arthritic hands. They watch the Reverend with little expression for this is not their first time.

The donkey shifts its weight and the cart rattles.

Mister Bob steps forward. He is crying tears through ageing tear ducts and his thin chest rattles like a lone umbrella in its stand.

Reverend Dickinson gestures to Mister Bob. "You'd best go in now, Mister Bob. And Mister Bob..?"

Mister Bob hesitates with his foot on the step of the porch.

"Thank you. Thank you for trying," Reverend Dickinson tells him.

Mister Bob manages to nod as he starts into the house like a man on the way to the gallows.

Reverend Dickinson, a soft film of dust already collecting on his glasses, nods toward a man who wears a dirty over-all and who wears a pair of odd boots. "Mister Sikes - will you do the honours please?"

Mister Sikes, clearing his throat, takes the bundle, places it on the rear of the cart and heads for the donkey.

The villagers stand idle, their frames bent in a sudden gust of wind, and observe as Mister Sikes leads the donkey and cart away, the body of the wrapped infant fragile in its space.

Reverend Dickinson turns to the gathered people. "There will be a Service at dusk. Let's leave Mary and Bob alone now, shall we?"

The villagers begin to wander off without a specific intent of going somewhere. There is no gossip, no whispers. They collect up their chairs and knitting and they go.

An elderly man, Mister Murray, wearing faded and patched English tweed and worn leather shoes, turns to Reverend Dickinson.

"May I have a quick, discrete word in your ear, Reverend? I suggest a chat with Mister Richards over there. It may already be too late -- the man has that look in his eyes. The internal light has been switched off, if you know what I mean." With that said, Mister Murray trails off into the flailing dust, the spoor left by the donkey cart already evaporating.

"Thank you, Mister Murray."

Mister Richards is pushing his hand-cart in the opposite direction of the street, toward the flatness of the wasteland.

"Mister Richards?"

Mister Richards hesitates. He waits for the Reverend to join him. "There isn't any use now is there, Reverend?" He enquires.

"I don't understand?"

"Any use in living, Reverend. In me, them, even you being here..."

"We are, at least, living, Mister Richards! If you cross that line, there is no coming back. You know this!"

Mister Richard peers down the barren street toward the hunched figures of the roaming villagers. "But there's nothing worth coming back for, Reverend. Is there?"

Reverend Dickinson wipes at the lenses of his spectacles, more in frustration than with reason.

"Mister Richards – there is always hope and a chance."

Mister Richards lifts the handles of his cart. "There is nothing, Reverend. Time we all realised that." With a grunt, he steps forward and points his beaked, veined nose toward the horizon and allows his cart to lead the way.

Deflated, Reverend Dickinson stands alone. He rocks on his heels. There was no use in arguing anymore. Words, like time, were spent. He glances up toward the lone hill to the East.

Joe has parked his truck, 'The Sow', on the same hilltop. He leans against the bonnet of the vehicle, viewing the town that God has forgotten below through a pair of binoculars. Dog squats on the ground nearby, flexing his huge wings, the carcass of a hare adding its seeping blood to the thirsty earth.

Joe can see Reverend Dickinson down there in the street, the white bundle on the rear of the donkey cart as it traipses toward an area outside the village. He pans the lenses over the houses, spots a wind-pump successfully straining to raise water from the depths. A person works in a field of weary corn. Joe focuses on the general dealer store, barely hesitating on the villagers that wander the street aimlessly. He settles the lens on the rudimentary hydroponics, the field of struggling beet and the two horses corralled beside it.

Joe lowers the binoculars. He pulls a silver tin from the pocket of his long coat and takes out a hand-rolled cigarette.

"A funeral looks like. Not good. And there's a priest. Even worse," he tells Dog.

Joe takes a match out of the tin.

"Funeral is a good hunting ground for a priest..."

Joe holds his right hand over the match. It ignites. No flint. No tricks. He lights the cigarette and flicks the match away.

"So my advice here is we go in and don't hang around. We buy what we need and get out and we try to avoid the priest."

He exhales a plume of smoke into the hot air.

The Fergusons' house is the only abode in the street that looks kept; that looks as if it contains life. It is a single story building, made from a salad of concrete blocks and timber. There is a bed of cacti near the front door, a stone walled outhouse and a garden fence that has seen better days. It stands directly opposite the Church.

In the rear garden there is a pigeon coop. The structure leans awkwardly on its four stilts. The coop's inhabitants are homing pigeons, messenger birds, and they flutter inconsistently in their confined space. They are all white in colour.

The front door opens and Sarah and Danya Ferguson step out. They are pushing a perambulator. Sarah is Danya's mother. She is middle-aged and her beauty is fading like the heels of the shoes she wears. Beneath the shade of the self-styled bonnet she wears, the darkness under her eyes speaks of restless nights; the tracks of time invade a greying hairline.

The same cannot be said for Danya, Sarah's daughter. Every story has, or is in need, of a Danya. She is the rose amongst the thorns. Her statue is lithe, the sureness of her limbs as certain as the grey flecked blue of her eyes, the barley colour of her pony-tailed hair entertaining sun spots. She is now your image. She is the youngest woman in the village.

Mother and daughter pause outside their house. The perambulator rocks on its ancient springs. Wandering villagers stop and view both mother and daughter with either hostility or longing. Momentarily, there is little movement in the street; like a sentence awaiting a punctuation mark.

Reverend Dickinson, polishing his glasses, senses this attitude. He notices the Ferguson family and hurries toward them.

But Danya is hesitating beside the perambulator outside her house. She is well aware of the atmosphere amongst the villagers that her and her mother's presence is causing. It troubles her.

"What is the matter, Danya?"

"Mother -- can we do this later? Please?"

Sarah, observing the approach of Reverend Dickinson, shakes her head. "No. It's Katherine's stroll time, Danya. Ten o'clock is her stroll time."

Reverend Dickinson arrives, his glances toward the rooted villagers enough to set them back into motion. His gaunt face lights up when he greets Danya, sobers when he acknowledges Sarah.

"Good morning, Danya. Sarah."

"Reverend Dickinson." Sarah's response is cold.

"Bob and Mary lost their child," the Reverend tells Danya, avoiding Sarah.

"That is sad. I'm very sorry."

Reverend Dickinson smiles quickly at Danya's sincerity.

"Don't apologize, Danya. A seed does not germinate in a crippled, arid soil. That is not Nature's way. We should know that by now. Am I right, Reverend?"

"We do what we must, Sarah."

"What rubbish! Let's walk Danya."

But Danya is looking down the street, toward the desert, the flat horizon. Something is attracting her attention; a sense of movement, of something out of the ordinary.

"Please, Sarah -- walking with the perambulator...it upsets everyone. Especially today..."

"It's Katherine's stroll time, Reverend. Danya! We will walk..."

Danya regains her composure and glances at the Reverend. "I am sorry about the baby," she tells him.

Hesitantly, Danya follows her mother into the street.

The graveyard is a sandy sprawl with no boundaries between it and the desert. Pieces of scrap wood have been tied together with rope to form a cross on each of the graves.

The body of the baby, wrapped in a swaddling, is taken off the cart by Mister Sikes. He does so with little emotion.

The Sow speeds across the sand toward the town of Erasmusville. Dog clings to his perch as he is thrown forwards and sideways. He hisses.

In the street, the breeze suddenly stiffens; picking up sand and pushing it for the sake of pushing it as it has nothing better to do.

In the graveyard, the sudden gust of wind disrespectfully throws sand at the mourners. They shield their faces as naturally as a person swats away a fly.

Danya and Sarah, pushing the perambulator, walk the street as the dust lifts about them like a petticoat attached to a temperamental air condition unit.

"Danya, cover Katherine. Quickly please!"

Danya leans into the pram and pulls up the knitted blanket.

"Hush! There, there..." Danya tells the occupant of the perambulator.

It is not a baby. It is not a human infant. It's a doll. It is a beautifully crafted, Victorian doll.

Danya glances up from the perambulator as she, again, senses this something; a vibration, perhaps? She looks toward the horizon, looks East.

"There! I knew I saw something," Danya exclaims.

She is looking down the street as The Sow appears, its silvery hue glistening with a halo effect. Joe is barely recognisable behind the windshield.

The Sow passes Danya and Sarah. The only sound offered by the vehicle is the rattling of the equipment in its rear. It whistles past them.

The Sow draws to a stop outside the general dealer, further up the street where a dust cloud briefly obscures it from Danya's view.

Joe climbs out of the vehicle, his long coat being tugged by the breeze. He hesitates as he makes eye contact with the few villagers that stand there. He absorbs their fragility, the frayed, tired material of an umbrella, the man wearing an odd pair of shoes, the faded colour of a man's shirt.

Dog remains in the truck's cabin with hooded eyes.

Joe makes eye contact with Mister Murray. There is a moment there in which Mister Murray finds himself consciously adjusting his tattered tie. Joe's smile is brief, but warm. Mister Murray ducks his head.

Joe enters the store, the heels of his leather boots firm on the gritted surface. Nobody follows him.

The general dealer is just that -- it trades anything from tinned food to coffins, second hand bicycles, and tattered novels. There is a chicken coop in the corner of the shop, the skeletal fowl content. A lone tomato plant struggles beneath a plastic canopy to grow its fruit.

Mister Harry, the Store's keeper, is staring at the stationary truck through the doorway, almost ignoring Joe. Mister Harry walks with the aid of a crutch.

"That's a good looking vehicle," Mister Harry tells the space between Joe and the doorway.

"Thanks."

"Not seen one like that before. Fact is, haven't seen a vehicle at all for some time now."

Joe hands over a slip of paper to Mister Harry. Joe's expression is soft, friendly. Mister Harry doesn't look at the piece of paper. Not yet.

"But of course you'd know that..." Mister Harry adds.

"Yes," answers Joe.

"...unless you been living in a hole in the ground. I don't have any fuel. No fuel. None whatsoever but you probably know that as well?"

"I know that."

Now Mister Harry looks Joe in the face. There is a quick intake of breath from Mister Harry. It is subtle, but it is there. It is a reaction one can associate to a man who sees an old friend who was presumed dead.

Joe absorbs the shop keeper's reaction without emotion.

"So how do you keep that on the road...with a wing and a prayer?" Mister Harry asks falteringly.

Joe's smile is quick. "Something like that," he replies.

"Do I know you?" Mister Harry asks Joe, his eyes averted.

"No."

Mister Harry nods to himself. He reads from the piece of paper in his hand. "Right then - let's see what I can help you with. Is this everything?"

"Yes. Thank you."

"I've got some canned pineapple? Six cans for a rabbit is the month's offer?"

"I'm good on pineapple. I have two rabbits to spare."

"You just want dynamite?"

"Yes. As much as you have I'll take."

Mister Harry kneels down behind the counter. He pushes aside some dented cans of pineapple revealing a squat Chubb safe. He works the mechanism.

"I've got sixteen sticks in stock. Not much need for dynamite anymore."

Joe looks through the open doorway, aware of the villagers that are watching him. Now becoming aware of Reverend Dickinson who, from across the street, is heading toward the general dealer, his Cossack floating in the breeze.

"Yes, as I thought, sixteen in total. No call for anything here anymore. Makes me wonder what you are doing here, Sir...?"

The voice that responds is nasal in tone, as if being delivered by a man wearing a mask and snorkel.

"Same thing all Diggers do, Mister Harry. They's all buying dynamite. Isn't that right? Only Diggers want dynamite."

Joe does not turn to face the voice.

He does not turn to study the three men that stand behind him. Their names are Hef, Sampson and Charles. These are the type that used to haunt your shopping malls or stand on your street corner. They are the type you wish Mother Nature did not forget. There is only one exception now. All the men are in their fifties. Sampson wears a hearing aid that may well have been invented in the era of the Beatles. The men are haggard, dirty, and clad in ill assorted garments ranging from a dinner jacket to a lengthy cashmere coat that trails on the ground.

"I thought I told you all to leave?" Mister Harry barks.

Hef points to Sampson's hearing aid. "Gather he didn't hear you, Harry."

"What you say?" Sampson asks with a dumb grin.

"We weren't talking to you anyway, Harry," advises Charles as he scratches his groin.

They've moved up the aisle, are checking Joe out closely. Charles is looking out of the doorway at The Sow. Immediately villagers drift back.

"We're talking to the Digger, Harry. We don't like Diggers. Diggers are from the dark like 'em flying rats and shit -- putting their thoughts in places we shouldn't be looking in is what my Mama told me. That's why we don't like Diggers," Hef says.

"Especially diggers with big birds what eat shit and brains," Charles adds.

Joe pulls a wad of stained dollar bills from his pocket. "How much do I owe you?" Joe asks Mister Harry.

Danya and Sarah, the perambulator in tow, arrive outside the general dealer. They are in time to hear the voice of Mister Harry emanating from within the building.

"That's money! I don't take money! I trade, you see. For food mainly and candles for a sheep and I'd give a whole lot more for a few rabbits -- a bicycle even..."

Danya recognises the arrival of Reverend Dickinson. There is a large crowd now. She swings her attention to the vehicle that she stands beside. She recognises its independence, the freedom it represents. She wants to touch the vehicle's hide, but refrains.

In the store, Joe scuffs his boots, a little embarrassed. "I've got two rabbits but I don't need a bicycle. Will they suffice?"

"Digger...we were talking to you!" Hef's nasal tone is suddenly sharp, like an exploding bubble.

"Digger's mothers are prostitutes, you know? Heard it said more than once. Da's you are bastards from the dark." That's from Sampson, his voice baritone.

Joe has yet to turnaround.

Joe's voice is very quiet. "Did I hear what I think you just said?"

"Not unless you're deaf..."

"Like me," scoffs Sampson.

Charles swings the skirt of his cashmere coat. "Is it true then? That your momma was a whore? Well, maybe you can trade the whore for..."

Now Joe turns. He looks them all in the face. He exudes calmness, a stillness that is transfixing and dangerous. He is seeing into them, sensing their weaknesses, and Hef, Sampson and Charles gradually show their discomfort. Hef shifts on his crooked knees. He glances at his friends. Both are transfixed by Joe's presence. Charles chews his lower lip.

It is suddenly quiet. Mister Harry doesn't move in the sudden silence. It is tangible.

Joe tilts his head a little. A quizzical smile appears on his lips, as if he has just discovered a secret after exploring a dark annex. He is staring at Sampson.

Sampson begins to urinate himself. The liquid wets the front of his trousers and soon trickles onto the dusty, concrete floor. Sampson pales. He is riveted by Joe's eyes, the aura he spreads.

Hef hears Sampson urinating. He barely manages to glance in that direction.

"Holy Shit," Hef whispers.

Mister Harry cannot see Joe's face. He can see only his back and Mister Harry realises that Joe has not moved a muscle in what has felt like an eternity.

Charles steps back. He has bitten into his lower lip. A spittle of blood flows. "Look...they were just words, okay? No harm meant. Okay?" He mumbles. He thumps Sampson's shoulder blades. "Stop pissing yourself, damn it!"

"Never ever insult the woman that gave a man the light of day."Joe's words fill the silence. He turns to exit the store.

"Sir...you forgot these," Mister Harry calls out, finally shaking himself out of his stupor.

"But I don't have anything to trade."

"There will be another time for that. Take the dynamite. I insist."

Joe collects up the dynamite. "I'll bring you rabbits. That is the deal. Thank you." He makes for the door, never looking at the three men.

Joe steps out into the sunlight. He sees Danya standing with Sarah, recognises Mister Murray as a battered umbrella held by a woman snaps in the breeze. He swings his attention back to Danya momentarily.

The exchange of looks between Joe and Danya is brief. But it is he that drops his look first. If Joe's look had lingered for two seconds more he would have seen the smile that touches the corners of Danya's eyes.

But Sarah has seen the moment and she digests it quietly.

As does Reverend Dickinson as he makes his way forward toward Joe.

"Out...the three of you. Out! And who is going to clean up that mess? Who, may I ask?"

The sound of Mister Harry's voice from within the store, snaps Joe back into reality. He heads for The Sow, Dog watching from his perch. He glances fleetingly at the perambulator that Sarah is unconsciously rocking.

Reverend Dickinson, his hand extended, suddenly blocks Joe's way.

"Welcome. The door to my Church is always open," the Reverend offers.

Joe feels the attention of the villagers boring into him. "Doesn't quite look that way to me, Reverend," he says quietly.

Joe gets into The Sow and the vehicle hums in response to his presence. Reverend Dickinson lowers his hand.

The Sow leaves the town to the West as quietly as when it first arrived. The silence its absence brings is quickly interrupted as Hef, Charles and Sampson step out of the store.

"What are you all looking at?" Hef asks the street. "Huh?" Hef grins when he spots Danya. He moves closer to her, villagers wary. "We'll get you one of these nights. Open you up like a ripe tomato," he tells Danya, his nasal tone causing her to flinch more than his body odour.

Danya glances to her mother."I want to go home now," she implores.

Sarah steps toe-to-toe with Hef. "You venture near my house and I will kill each and every one of you," she warns Hef through gritted teeth. Then she notices that Danya is leaving, heading for her house. Sarah grabs the perambulator and hurries after her daughter. "Danya, will you wait up?"

Hef glares at Sampson, ignoring the people around him. "You stink!"

"What?"

Hef marches away, Sampson, bow-legged, and Charles following.

Reverend Dickinson hasn't budged. He keeps his focus on the distant dust trail left by The Sow.

"Morning, Reverend," says Mister Harry from the porch.

"What is it, Mister Harry?"

"I know his face."

Reverend Dickinson makes eye contact with the store keeper who stands on the porch. "You know him?"

"I don't know *him*. But I knew his father. That I am sure."

CHAPTER SIX

The terrain The Sow travels is familiar -- we remember it from the beginning, before The Event, when bees still had pollen to gather. It is now just desert. A single skeleton of a wind turbine stands aloof on the hilltop, boasting a shadow of futility.

The dirt track carves its way between two hills, a bend approaching.

Joe slams on the brakes and Dog falls about the seat then regains his balance. Slowly Joe gets out of the cabin. He pauses alongside the bonnet, tilting his head into the sun to view the structure that dominates the area.

It is a monument. It is an 'upside' down *V*. It stands, Eiffel Tower like, some sixty foot high and thirty foot across at the base. The structure is made from the wrecks of motor vehicles – bonnet is welded to trunk, trunk welded to bonnet.

There are Toyotas and Chevrolets, a Ford or two and even a Mercedes. Banks of sand have cluttered the base of the structure, forced there by wind and the elements.

Joe walks under the Monument and lights a roll-up; lights the match the way he always does. He peers up into the belly of the monument. There's a plaque to his left so he wanders over to it.

Joe reads aloud from the plaque. "The Mechanics' Monument to the God in the Sky -- in memory of our Mister David Erasmus...in defeat there is success."Joe hesitates. He runs a finger over the name of David Erasmus. He nods his head then walks away from the monument, his boots kicking up fine grains of dust. He squats on his haunches, studies the structure, the flatness of the surrounding land.

In The Sow, Dog shuffles on his perch.

"Twenty years is a long time to remain defeated. But I'm pleased. I'm pleased that you existed, father," Joe tells the Monument.

Joe passes his hand over a few inches of the ground beside him. It's a calm and soothing gesture. He allows his hand to hover momentarily. Then he repeats the action. He flicks his cigarette away.

"But not here. Here you don't exist," he tells the soil.

He stands and heads back to The Sow, the Monument towering over him. He gets in and settles in the driver's chair.

"That's his monument, Dog. The man lived. That's the positive. The negative is that it's all negative -- not a whisper of life anywhere. No life in the dead."

Joe kicks The Sow into gear, turns up the music.

"Not even a sigh," he concludes and drives forward.

In the pigeon coop, Sarah catches a bird -- it is white. She exits the coop, holds the bird aloft and let's it free. Her actions are in no way clandestine. She shields her eyes against the sun as she watches the pigeon circle.

The bird circles the town as it gains its bearings, then flies west where the sun is yet to settle. Travelling with the bird, the desolate, uninhabited land stretches below. The footprint Mother Nature has left in her wake is as solemn as it is vast.

Then we see a pinprick of movement. It is Mister Richards pushing his hand-cart. He's as diminutive as an ant on the landscape. The pigeon flies on.

Mister Richards is approaching the top of a small hill. A cemetery stands there, its clutter of tombstones prominent, like the ivory of a broken piano's keyboard. At the nearest end of the cemetery, there's a gate. It is made from wrought iron.

Mister Richards, his armpits saturated with sweat, approaches the gate. He hesitates there, an uncertainty reflected in his posture. Carved into the gate, images of death and agony leer back at him. With trepidation, he pushes his hand-cart forward toward the crest of the hill.

There he again hesitates as he looks down on the Trader's Village.

You are looking down on a carbon copy of Erasmusville. The geography of the single street, the shacks either side of it, is duplicated. You notice that the village is better maintained, that there seem to be more people walking its street. Then you become conscious of the fairground. It has been erected on the edge of the town. It boasts an antiquated merry-go-round, a Ferris wheel and a dodgem car track.

You notice too that the elderly people, who inhabit this town, wear their finest clothing. You glimpse a dinner suit and even a ball gown. They are an ill fitting but fond memory.

Whilst Mister Richards makes his way toward the village, you become attuned to the fact that, though the sun is ultra bright, an eerie darkness, a shadow, hangs over the Trader's Village. There is no physical reason for this. No cloud, nothing solid to obstruct the sun's rays. It is just there, like a fog, a thing; an invisible carpet of gloom.

A mature couple ride on the antiquated merry-go-round. Distorted fairground music invades the air. They are holding hands. Their faces do not show the thrill of the ride; rather they reflect the mood of monotony, of travelling in a circle that has no conclusion other than death. That is the reason they are there. That is the purpose of the fairground.

Mister Witherspoon who wears a fake rose in his buttonhole, hurries toward the merry-go-round. He is rotund and he expertly makes his way through the gathered crowd.

He comes to a stop.

"Hello, Sky. It's me."

The man Mister Witherspoon addresses is in his early twenties. He's handsome in a James Dean sort of way and supports this by wearing the similar fashion. He is pale, almost anaemic, in complexion. There is a dangerous fragility to Sky; a fragility that, you sense, he would go to great lengths to protect, no matter the cost.

"I can see that Mister Witherspoon."

Mister Witherspoon catches his breath. "Yes of course you can."

"Is the funeral over?"

"Yes. Sad really -- Rose was a nice woman. Very considerate," Mister Witherspoon offers.

Sky watches the merry-go-round. "Time is a mean fucker, Mister Witherspoon. It waits for no one. You have the list?" He asks.

Mister Witherspoon withdraws a sheet of paper from his pocket, as well as a woman's wrist-watch. He hands them over to Sky, who pockets the watch, opens the sheet of paper.

The white homing pigeon flies toward the Church in the Trader's village. It is a replica of the building that stands in Erasmusville, except it has a solid, observatory shape dome clinging to it like a growth, a tumour.

Alongside the dome, a pigeon coop, its occupants all dark in colour. The pigeon, sent by Sarah, comes to roost on the roof of the coop.

Sky lifts his head from reading the note. "Not much to leave behind after seventy-six years, is it Mister Witherspoon? A candelabra and a collection of Chinese jade..?"

"No. I'm afraid not," Mister Witherspoon whispers, embarrassed.

"Barely pays for her keep or her husband's."

Sky's attention shifts. He has spotted Hef, Sampson and Charles near the Ferris wheel. They are gesturing for Sky to join them. Three under-nourished horses stand near the three men.

Sky pockets the slip of paper. "Keep an eye on Mister Franks in car nine. He's looking a fraction pale there. He, at least, owns a decent stamp collection."

Mister Witherspoon watches Sky walk off. "Right," Mister Witherspoon tells no-one in particular.

As Sky approaches Hef, Sampson and Charles, he wrinkles his nose. "You stink," he tells them.

Sampson stares at the ground.

"We got news to trade, Mister Sky," Hef says.

"Important news," Charles adds.

"Sampson pissed himself. Tell him! Go on..."

"I saw...I saw...in his eyes..."

"...like a deep tunnel with no end, right...?" Hef offers.

Sampson nods his head vigorously. "Yes. Yes. That's it - no end."

Sky shifts his weight on his feet. "He's a Digger?" He asks quietly.

Hef nods like a dog shaking off water.

"Was she there? Did she see him?"

Charles nods at Sky, his grin baring teeth the colour of soot.

"Go back. Watch. Don't cause your usual mayhem. Just watch," Sky informs the three men.

Hef steps forward. "What's the trade, Mister Sky?"

Sky looks over to the Dodgem cars. He singles out a pale faced man who is in the process of being rammed by another dodgem car. The man is wide-eyed and trembling.

Sky looks at Hef. "Any of you scum a keen philatelist?"He asks.

CHAPTER SEVEN

Joe stands in the centre of the canyon we remember so well. The Sow is parked at the entrance. The sun is beginning to drop in the sky and the vehicle reflects the changing light like a chameleon.

The canyon has changed. There are no saplings, no tufts of grass, and the soil is now the colour of white chalk. Dog is perched on the curve of a boulder, his head askew, watching Joe as Joe scuffs the surface of the earth with the well worn toe of his boot. Joe crouches and peers beneath a boulder.

Sky hurries up the street in the Trader's village. He is about to pass Mister Richards who is heading toward the fairground area. A layer of dust now covers the contents of Mister Richard's hand-cart, the soft baby toy limp with the weight of the dust.

"Excuse me...? I've just arrived. Where do I go?"

Sky glances at the contents of the cart. He points toward the fairground. "Ask for Mister Witherspoon...that chair French?"

"Yes. It was my wife's."

Sky sees the soft toy. He snaps it up. "I'll take this as deposit. Okay?"

"If you say so," Mister Richards replies, his tone one of defeat.

Sky offers a smile. "I do. Welcome."

Sky hurries toward the Church but just before he enters the building, he looks across the street where an identical replica of the Ferguson house stands. The windows and the doors are bolted. Sky glances over the house with a sense of pride, almost gloating. He turns and enters the Church.

There's less daylight within the building, coldness even in the harsh sunlight. Sky heads toward the covered altar, veers off and enters a narrow, bare hallway. He moves forward and enters a stark, semi-circular room. Its only furniture is a wooden desk and a chair. Leading off this room, is an archway -- behind the arch, a room of darkness. There is a doorway to the side.

Sky enters that doorway. He pauses there, tosses the soft toy toward the bed in the centre of the room.

"There's a Digger in Erasmusville," he tells the man resting on the bed. The man rolls over and looks at Sky. His name is Trader. He is a soul shrunk in a once tall frame. He is the dead alive.

"I know. I heard. But it is yet to be proven."

Sky lies down on the bed. He embraces Trader, like a child would his father.

"I was told..."

"...nothing. You were told nothing," Trader interrupts. "Those three faeces eating, unwashed doggery couldn't tell left from right, right from wrong. Their breath alone will taint you, Sky. Let me smell."

"You want to what?"

"Let me smell!"

Sky exhales into Trader's face, their lips close. Trader sniffs.

"It is as tainted as the day's dawn. Deceit is contagious."

Sky sits up on the bed. "But there is a chance? I mean -- that this man could be a Digger?"

Trader holds out a well manicured hand. "Rose Jarvis. She died?"

"Sorry, I forgot..."

Sky pulls out the ladies wrist-watch and hands it over. Trader caresses Sky's hand before he takes the timepiece. He gets out of the bed and puts on a robe that hangs like an old curtain over a once proud window.

"She met with him," Sky informs Trader.

"They copulated?"

"No. Of course they didn't!"

Sky follows Trader into the lounge. Trader walks toward the archway and enters the dark area.

"Then their meeting was of no consequence to me," Trader says as he disappears into the black.

"You mean to us - it was of no consequence to us. Am I right?" Sky's voice is suddenly shrill, like that of a spoilt child. He steps closer to the archway, but does not enter."To your promise to me, remember?"

Trader's voice is soft in the darkness. "Yes, my promise, my trade for pleasures past." Then he raises his voice. "Yes, my promise to you."

Sky calms as he watches a soft light invade the room. It is the light from a night's sky pregnant with stars. As this light grows, Sky is able to see Trader operating the winch attached to the curved wall. Trader is mechanically opening the roof of the dome.

Trader pauses in his action to look at Sky. "But only when she is with child. Best you never forget that, my infertile friend," he tells Sky.

"You have to do that, don't you? Just keep ramming it home like vomit in reverse. That's what gets you off?"

Trader turns his back on Sky. "No my sweet boy," he says. "You do."

Joe moves through the canyon. Neither torchlight nor lamp is required. Above him, the stars seem so close he could touch them. He squats, looks at the ground.

"If he is true to his gift," Trader tells Sky, "then he will, at first, work at night. He will have no need for light. After all, what he searches for is already buried in the dark."

The damp light of the night's sky fills the dome, ricocheting off the hundreds of timepieces that hang together like crystal drops on a chandelier. Wrist watches of all sizes, age and shape, their mechanisms still, hands dormant, stalled at different times. Every time-piece hangs from a thin thread. They seem to be floating in the air, these souvenirs of the dead.

Trader begins to feed a thread into the strap socket of the watch Sky has just given him. "He won't tempt to unearth anything," Trader continues. "He'll simply probe -- he'll feel. Touch and sense. Let his presence be known -- that he's a friend, a new light, a respectful visitor."

Joe sweeps both his hands under the belly of a rock. The muscles across his hands are taut. He moves on like a water diviner, his stride loose, calm and sure footed on the terrain.

Trader randomly touches a free floating watch. "If a Digger has a response, he'll settle and make camp. He'll open the way for the dead to speak. He's as patient as a vulture. No difference between them really -- both eat off the dead...travel the same road."

"He's got a bird with him. An ugly bird," Sky offers.

Trader sends the wristwatch aloft. It swings like a pendulum. "That's interesting. I wasn't aware."Trader looks at Sky. "A Digger is patient and sensitive -- potent weaponry in the battle for love, Sky. Do you think you are capable?"

Sky stiffens in the doorway. “Screw you, Trader. I shared your bed, now she will share mine.”

“And what of me, Sky? What of us?”

Sky turns his back. “A trade is a trade. That’s what you always tell me.”

Trader hears Sky leave. He smiles, the night sky reflecting in his oval glasses.

Joe lets his hands roam at the base of a boulder, where dirt meets rock.

Suddenly, a few slivers of loose stone and a few grains of sand float toward Joe’s hand, and cling onto his flesh. Like a magnet draws iron shavings.

He brushes off the slivers of stone and moves on.

A suspended watch begins to swing, to bob up and down. It touches another watch. That, too, begins to move.

Trader observes, doesn’t move, and listens to the metallic rustle, like a breeze through a wind-chime.

Joe focused, shifts a hand to his left, to his right. He rotates on his heels, pirouetting almost, palms an inch or two off the ground. The occasional sliver of flint or dust rises and sticks to his hands. Concentrated, resolute energy as he rotates on his heels. His muscles are taut; a ballet in the moonlight.

Trader watches as a few timepieces shift now -- spin on their axis. Not all of them. A few -- like dancing puppets on invisible strings. Above them the night sky through the open dome.

"Thank you father," Trader tells the night sky.

Almost feline, Joe ceases his movement. He squats on the earth, his chest inflating, deflating as the slivers of stone and dust slip off his hands.

CHAPTER EIGHT

Reverend Dickinson stumbles into the arched sanctuary of his Church. He is drunk. He drinks from a bottle of white liquid, compliments of Mister Needham who manages to distil the juices from rancid potatoes that are beyond being edible.

The night's light barely intrudes through the cracked, smeared plastic sheeting covering the windows, silhouetting the few chairs in the room and the bulk of the makeshift altar.

His eyes move around the room. "Where are you? Where are you? Are you in here?" He looks in the vestry. "I know you're here somewhere..."

He looks under a chair on wobbly knees. "Under here? No."

He stands in the centre of the aisle facing the rear of the church. "Come out, come out, wherever you are," he calls. The only response he gets is the wet echo of his own voice of the walls. He pulls up a chair with his foot and sinks into like deadweight.

"O come all ye faithful joyful and triumphant, O come ye, O come ye to Bethlehem. Come and behold Him, born the King of Angels..."

He stops singing and remains still for a moment. He senses a presence behind him. Slowly he turns and looks up at the dirty, broken stain-glass window above him at the far end of the church. The window depicts God on high with his subjects kneeling at his feet. The images are childishly etched in crayon, a gift by a woman long deceased.

"There you are," he sneers. He glares at the window. "Why, why must you torture me this way? I your most loyal servant, this is my reward? To fornicate, to screw, to fuck! Thank you for that little joke, Messiah!"

He tries to stand but thinks better of it. "Am I not a man of God but a man of flesh and blood also? Made in your own image? Imperfect image! Ungracious Idol! I will kneel to you no more."

He sits quietly for a moment, looks across to the empty chairs that are his only company. "They sit here, frail and weak, the dying and the already dead, and you ask me to lie - to tell them their suffering in this world will be their salvation in the next. I made a vow to love only you and this how you re-pay me? Hell and damnation?" He stares at his feet. "I accuse you of hypocrisy Blessed Lord, who did punish the meek and murder the innocent. Hypocrite! Vile hypocrite! Prophet of doom! Do you have anything to say in your defence? No? Then the sentence is guilty, guilty as charged."

He staggers to his feet, the bottle slipping from his fingers. It breaks with a dull, useless thud.

"Why did you not stop us? Not one word," he asks the walls. "Not much to ask was it - a child, a product of love? Not much. No."

He burps and laughs out aloud because of it.

"But she was sorry. Danya said she was sorry...my sweet Danya," he tells the sound of plastic flapping on the roof.

Across the street from the Church, the light of candle flickers in a window of the Ferguson house.

The interior of the house reminds you of the house your grandmother may have built. Its furnishings are sparse but selective; heavy furniture inexpertly refurbished and prints of a once popular Monet and a Picasso, a Warhol, nailed to a wall; all somehow salvaged and badly repaired, collected after The Event like driftwood on a beach after a storm. The walls are a mismatch of brick, rock and wood. It is a sad attempt of making a home, but at least it is an attempt.

Sarah, carrying a pitcher of steaming water, enters the bathroom. Danya is in the bath. It is a metal tub and she sits with her knees up. There is no running water. Danya's thoughts are elsewhere.

"Here we go. Perfect temperature, the way you like it," Sarah says as she enters. "What were you thinking about?"

"Why I hate this wind and the dust. It clings to me like a snake's skin. I think the dust is trying to throttle us, to starve us from breathing."

Sarah kneels beside Danya and pours the water over her hair and upper body.

"It's a wind from hell, I say. At least, before, it was cooler and the children would float paper bags on pieces of string. One day we'll see that again."

"There was no dust on the automobile," Danya points out. "No dust. Not even a dead insect. Not a fly, a locust. Did you notice?"

"No I didn't."

"I thought, perhaps, that he came from somewhere where there is no dust, no insects but that's impossible, isn't it?"

"Oh, so you were thinking about that man!" Sarah teases as she begins to sponge Danya.

"I was not!"

"Calm down. No need to be defensive, Danya. To be honest, I'd be thinking about him *if* he had looked at me the way he looked at you."

"I don't know what you mean."

Sarah's hands are working Danya's shoulders, gently and sensuously. "I think you do," Sarah whispers in her daughter's ear. Sarah's hands begin to explore Danya's chest. Danya tenses her body, raises her knees tighter to her breasts, but then she leans back, closing her eyes.

Sarah leans closer to her daughter's ear. "A man like that carries a scent that fills your senses with wicked abandonment; makes you imagine places to run, places to hide and to meet. Did you see his hands? They were strong, very strong hands that could hurt, just a little, but in the right places."

Sarah leans over the bath a little further, her chin resting on Danya's wet shoulder.

"Mother..."

"Hush."

Then Danya screams. She screams at the small window in the wall ahead of her.

Hef has his face glued to the outside of the bathroom window, working his tongue like a snake's. He licks the pane of glass.

"Get a robe on!" Sarah shouts to Danya.

Sarah charges into the passageway and into the bedroom. From under the bed, in a smooth action, she collects the twelve bore shotgun that has seen better times. Now she returns down the passageway and enters the kitchen. She swings open the kitchen door in time to...

...see Charles crossing the small garden near the shed. Sarah fires the shotgun and its pellets blast into the shed as Charles "yelps" and sprints around the corner of the house, his cashmere coat trailing like linen in the wind.

Sarah staggers under the recoil of the weapon.

"Stay where you are, Danya!" She shouts.

Sarah steps away from the kitchen door and into the garden. Hef comes sprinting from around the corner, straight towards her. Hef skids to a halt, his arms fluttering like a windmill. Sarah trains the gun on him.

"Did he send you?"

Hef shakes his head.

"Then run away you idiot," Sarah tells him.

Hef does as Sarah shoots a round harmlessly into the night sky. She heads back into the house as she loads a thick cartridge. She storms into the lounge where she opens the only window in time to...

...see Sampson making a bee-line for the small, crooked gate. Sarah fires again, the pellets dancing in the sand near the running man. Sampson is over the fence and into the street, swallowed up by the darkness.

"Bugger it!"Curses Sarah. "Danya, where are you?"

"In the bathroom," Danya replies, her voice shaking.

Sarah sets the gun aside and takes a deep breath. Then she hurries down the passageway and into the bathroom. Danya is huddled in the corner wearing a robe.

"Have they gone?"

"Yes. Be calm now. Come here. Come."

Danya settles into Sarah's hug, her body trembling slightly. "Why can't they just leave me alone? Why?"

"Ignorant fools. It will never happen again. I will always protect you."

"That is what Reverend Dickinson promised!" Danya says as she steps back from her mother.

"I know. And he'll hear from me first thing in the morning. Trust me."

CHAPTER NINE

Dawn does not break gently since The Event. It cleaves the night away with its heat and offers no respite between day and night.

Joe squats behind a boulder for protection midway up the canyon. He is attaching two fuse wires to a makeshift detonator. He does so with expertise.

Dog is perched beside him, the vulture preening itself. Joe leans over and he strokes Dog under his chin.

"Could be that he is buried too deep, could be that he's not. But then I wouldn't be feeling anything. But I am," Joe tells Dog. "But it's not a true feeling. Just not right -- as if someone blew out his candle with a breath that was not his own. There's just an uninvited dark left Dog, and that isn't good, my friend. It's an angry dark that can swallow a man up and have him lose his way forever. So let's see if a bit of added light may help."

Joe drives down the plunger on the detonator, ducks his head.

A beat as the canyon lies still as the sun weans itself of its brief redness.

The force of the blast is sufficient to topple a few boulders and raise a good plume of dust.

In that moment, as you look through the rising, unsettled dust cloud toward the mouth of the canyon, you see the shapes of four horsemen. The image reminds you of that time in the canyon, of the man and his fob watch, the whine of the final bullet.

Joe, higher up in the canyon, clears the dust from around his face, coughs, and surveys the outcome of the blast. Dog hisses. Joe's jaw tightens as he spots the horsemen.

Sky is mounted on one of the horses. He wears jodhpurs, riding boots and a tweed hacking jacket, all attire inherited from the dead. Behind him, slouched in their saddles, are Hef, Charles and Sampson.

"Hello," Sky shouts, his voice signing off the canyon walls.

Dog shifts on his rock, agitated.

Joe glances at Dog. "My sentiments exactly, Dog."

Joe turns his back on the intruders to survey the aftermath of his explosion. He goes straight to the area between the two boulders were he placed the dynamite. There's a hole three feet deep there now. He gets on his knees.

"I'm asking permission to come aboard, Captain?"

"Depends who's asking?" Joe responds.

Sky dismounts, his clean riding boots getting a good wash of dust. "Stay on your horses, all of you. You caused enough chaos last night. Next time I hope she shoots to kill," Sky warns Hef and his friends. Hef spits on the ground in response and Sky grimaces.

Sky begins to make his way into the canyon, glancing over The Sow and Joe's camp. There's a canvas bivouac, a circle of rocks shielding last night's fire and a few pots and pans neatly hung from a makeshift rack. The salted skin of a hare cures on the face of a rock.

"My name is Sky."

Joe ignores Sky's offer of a handshake and this brings a fleeting smile to Sky's lips.

"We're sort of neighbours," explains Sky.

"You're from Erasmusville?"

"No. I'm from the Trader's village maybe twelve miles to the West. Bit more life there, more stimulation. You should visit us sometime."

"Maybe I will."

Sky is looking at Dog as Joe keeps his distance. "Rumour has it you're a Digger?"

"Rumour has it I may be just like that lizard over there and looking under a rock for shade. What do you and those three idiots want?" Joe asks.

"The diamonds aren't here, you know."

"Who said anything about diamonds?"

Sky avoids Joe's eyes. He puts the toe of his boot on a rock and wipes the dust. "You're a Digger, aren't you? That's what you do - scavenge for rich flotsam. Last one that came here was maybe eight or nine years ago. The old folk found him in the boulders screaming that he had a noise in his head."

Joe doesn't move. "I'll remember that - not to start screaming I mean."

Sky begins to polish his other boot. "But then, maybe the guy who went mad wasn't what people are saying you really are. If you know what I mean?"

"No. I don't know what you mean."

Sky makes the mistake of looking Joe in the eyes now; perhaps to prove his strength, his status. The warning in Joe's eyes is plain – step away, boy, before you drown.

Sky, flustered, puts his boot back on the ground, squares his back. He refers to Dog. "That's an ugly bird. Ugliest I've ever seen."

" Are you done here? I've got work to do."

" A man I know -- he says to tell you that he knows about the wall – why it's there...reticent is what he said. That's the word - reticent."

"I know what it means. Did he say why?"

Sky shrugs. "Best you come ask him yourself when you're not so busy. I'll be seeing you. West, twelve miles and drive safely. Traffic is hell these days."

Sky chuckles to himself as he turns away. Then he turns back. "One last thing --which way did you come in from?"

"East..."

"And...?"

Joe shrugs. "The sun still rises."

For a moment Sky looks vulnerable. "That figures," he says softly, but then he shrugs it off and navigates his way down through the boulders.

Joe watches Sky head back to the horses. Hef, Charles and Sampson are sitting forward in their saddles, watching him.

Joe turns his back on them.

Sarah Ferguson looks through the gap in her lounge curtains. She watches the fair sized group of villagers that are making their way into the Church, some forever bent against an expected breeze.

Sarah hears the kitchen door open and close in the house and she hurries into the kitchen and looks through the window.

She's in time to see Danya, wearing trousers and heavy boots, exit the rear garden via a rickety gate that is near the pigeon coop.

Sarah takes a deep breath. She smiles as she exhales. She collects her bonnet off the sideboard and leaves the kitchen, closing the door behind her.

Reverend Dickinson, in the Church, surveys the congregated villagers. He winces as he watches Sarah enter through the main door. She takes her place to the rear of those already seated, aloof.

Reverend Dickinson raises a hand to silence the murmur. "Last night, the Fergusons were attacked," he announces. "Yes, whilst we lay in our beds, those three Heathen scum, employees of the Trader, tried to enter their house, to...to violate..."

"Rape! The word is rape...tried to rape Danya, Reverend," interrupts Sarah, her voice domineering. "And if any one of those viral infected scum were to touch my Danya, then my daughter and I would have no option but to pack our meagre belongings and seek protection from Trader."

A wave of discomfort ripples through the congregation.

Reverend Dickinson again raises his hand. "We will not permit that to happen."

"Just who are we? Do you mean the people in this room? For pity's sake, wake up! I want a police force. I want men to protect my home," Sarah orders before leaving the Church, the door closing behind her with a dull thud.

There's an abrupt silence.

"Mister Harry - you are the mayor?" Reverend Dickinson finally asks a frail, spectacled man.

"Yes...but...so many years since we had police, Reverend. Must be at least..."

"What we need is that nice young man that was here yesterday..." interrupts a woman who wears a plastic raincoat. "He can do it."

Reverend Dickinson takes a deep breath. "The stranger is not our concern. It is our duty to protect Danya -- our promise. Mister Harry -- a police force...?"

Mister Harry squirms beneath the sudden attention. "I do still have the uniforms and the hats. Somewhere, I think."

There's an audible, collected sigh of relief from the congregation as Reverend Dickinson struggles to hide his apprehension by brushing dust of the pulpit that leans at a peculiar angle.

CHAPTER TEN

The sound of the crowbar Joe uses to shift rock echoes in the canyon. He is sweating and he's removed his shirt. Nearby, a small fire burns over which roasts a dead rabbit. A can of pineapple and a water canteen show that a meal is due.

Dog preens himself as Joe digs the crowbar deeper beneath an obstinate rock.

"...not idle chatter. No, Dog. Looking and wanting something," Joe mumbles to Dog. "Why come to me like a blue-fly to a mound of dung? A man has a problem where he is and what he does, he makes a change, right? Every road has a detour; go left, go right, go straight. That is his choice." Exasperated, Joe sits down on a boulder, wags a finger at Dog. "Just don't make it my problem. Especially that sort. Sky - who is called Sky? Isn't there enough sky? There's nothing but negative oozing from him like an old car battery. Just like this place, Dog. Negative."

Joe lifts his head. "Come on! Speak to me!" He suddenly shouts.

Dog ruffles his feathers as Joe's words bounce back off the rock. Then silence.

As if in abeyance, a sod of chalky earth topples near where Joe was digging.

Joe hears the movement of the falling sod of earth, looks to it. He grins. "Apologies for the shouting, fine stuff," he tells the soil.

Joe drops to his knees and begins digging with his bare hands. He soon reveals a glimpse of black material. It is wedged like a layer in a sandwich. He pulls at the material. It won't budge so he gives it another jerk and applies more strength. He leans back on his heels.

The material suddenly gives and pops out the hole. Joe falls back on his backside. Attached to the remnants of the material are the well preserved, skeletal remains of a human hand.

You can barely recognise the colour of this material, but you finally do. It is the colour of the clothing worn by the armed, mounted Border Patrol.

Dog reacts by flapping his huge wings, the downdraft causing a cloud of dust.

I am Dog. We both seek a carcass.

Joe collects himself and kneels alongside the remains. There's an edge of excitement to him as he blows away the dust, scrapes away the congealed soil, revealing more of the fingers and the wrist bone.

Joe rocks on his haunches and looks at Dog. "It's time for my silence now Dog. But you listen to me now and listen well, my friend. If I don't come back, you eat me true and clean. You hear me, Dog? You finish me before the worms do. True and clean is what I ask for."

Dog stares and offers a blink from hooded eyes.

He seeks his for a different reason.

Joe takes a deep breath. "Good, Dog -- good. Yes, before the worms get me and before the Priest gets to me."

From his trouser pocket, Joe pulls out a strip of leather -- it is plaited, like a fake dog's bone -- and he puts it between his teeth, and chews down on it so it becomes an extension of his mouth. He gets comfortable on his haunches, settles his feet on the ground, ensuring his boots grip the earth's crust. He's planting himself.

Joe bites down on the strip of leather with force.

The dark feathered pigeons in Trader's coop flutter in panic as he snatches one out of the air. He holds the bird, calming it, stroking it with his manicured fingers before opening the door and releasing it. A flutter of wings snapping in the sunlight as the pigeon takes flight.

You are able, through the gap between the two boulders, to see the man who is hunched over what you mistakenly think is a pile of garbage, of plastic. Out of the corner of your eye you take notice of the size of the bird that sits as stoic as a statue.

You see the naked back of the man. His shoulders are broad and glisten with sweat. You inhale quickly as you see the muscles on the man's back tense and ripple. You hold your breath as those same muscles remain taut. Your reaction is alien to you and you are confused by it.

You shift your position silently for a better view. Now you see that his hands are hovering over what you think is garbage, plastic. Every sinew in the man seems to be working. He rotates his body and his chest suddenly expands with a breath of air or is it shock? That thing between his teeth - he is gnawing on it, his jawbones set rigid.

You are trying to hold your own breath.

There is a tremble to his hovering fingers.

You exhale and 'yelp' simultaneously as the man is suddenly thrown backwards as if kicked by an invisible horse, a something. You clutch your mouth to stiffen any further noise as the man is slammed against the ground.

There he remains motionless.

Sarah Ferguson's face lights up like a lighthouse on a foggy night as she watches Trader's black pigeon settle on her own pigeon coop. The bird carries no written message. There is no need. It is a message in itself, understood by Sarah.

Sarah bites back her frustration when she hears Reverend Dickinson calling her name.

"I'm over here, Reverend," she answers.

Reverend Dickinson appears around the corner of the house. Three men trail behind him. The men are wearing the uniforms of the Border Patrol, and they do not fit the men at all. The clothes hang like wet dishcloths on the men's frail, ageing frames.

"I thought I'd let you know, Mister Chalmers, Meyers and Conrad have volunteered. We now have three policemen," Reverend Dickinson announces with some pride, his spectacles clear of fine dust.

"They look like retired clowns, Reverend. Are they armed?"

"Armed?"

"Guns, Reverend - weapons. Have you not asked yourself why those heathen scum as you aptly name them, are taking a renewed interest in my daughter?"

"You think because of the arrival of the stranger?"

"Danya's importance to this community is no secret, Reverend."Sarah looks at the three men. "Do you have guns?"

"Mister Harry has a rifle I think," Mister Chalmers finally offers, his withered neck shrunk in the collar of the uniform.

"Then off you go," Sarah orders the men and they do so without debate.

The Reverend nods after the retreating men. "They will watch this house every night and keep you safe."

"Keep Danya safe, Reverend."

"Yes, that is what I mean." Reverend Dickinson spots the dark pigeon as it struts on the roof of the coop. "That's an unusual colour?"

"Yes. Yes it is. A mongrel, I suppose: a little mix-up of genes. The result of forced copulation, but you know all about that, don't you?" Sarah responds, watching the Reverend physically wince against her words.

Reverend Dickinson inhales. "I was wondering if I may speak with Danya."

"About?"

"Well, organizing a liaison with the stranger -- discussing the importance of such a liaison. Perhaps we can talk over a cup of tea?"

"I'd thought something a little stronger than tea, might appease, Reverend?"

Reverend Dickinson looks down at his feet, Sarah's verbal nips draining him of any further courage.

"Danya rode out at dawn Reverend to meet with the stranger."

Reverend Dickinson lifts his head, unable to hide his joy. "But why didn't you tell me? This is good news! If she were to like the man...to fall in love with him...that would even be better news, but, 'slowly-slowly' as they say when it comes to matters of the heart."

"Who said anything about love, Reverend? I never did. They will fornicate. He will impregnate. Love will NEVER enter the equation. Never..."

The Reverend reacts as if he's been slapped in the face not once, but twice. "You seriously can't mean that, Sarah! Danya is a young woman, he a young man! Their union, their meeting must be honest and real. God knows this community desires this..."

"Frankly, God knows pooh around here, Reverend," Sarah interrupts. "Look around you, or has the dust and the dying and your nightly intake of home brew finally blinded you? You leave Danya to me."

"Sarah -- we must discuss this! Please?"

"The matter is closed, Reverend."

The kitchen door slamming concludes the conversation. Reverend Dickinson stands like a ship lost at sail, his only company a dark pigeon that struts with metallic sounds on the roof of the pigeon coop.

CHAPTER ELEVEN

A shadow passes over Joe as he lies on the ground. He stirs, eyes blinking -- in his mouth he still bites down on the leather strip. It takes him a second or two to identify the person that looms over.

Her hair cascades down either side of her face and it shades her eyes, highlighting their shape and colour. She moves away, the loss of her shadow allowing the sun back into his eyes.

"Where did you go?" She asks him.

He sits up. He's no longer sweating but the dust clings to his torso. He sees that she is standing beside Dog - is stroking the bird and that Dog is calm beneath her hand.

He removes the leather strip from his mouth. "Here. I was here," he tells her.

She smiles, accepting the lie. "I thought you were dead. But then I saw you were breathing. When I sleep, I close my eyes. You don't."

He gets to his feet. "I wasn't sleeping."

She holds his look. "No, I didn't think you were. I brought you some water from your camp. What is your name?"

"Joe."

"Just 'Joe'?"

"Just 'Joe.'"

"My name is Danya. Danya Ferguson. I live in Erasmusville but you already know that."

"Yes."

She tries not to look at his bare chest, the muscles of his stomach and, instead, strokes Dog's head who, if he were a cat, would begin to purr.

He hides his smile, a little uncertain as to where or what to do next.

"Is he your pet?" She asks.

"A little more than that," he replies. "We hunt together."

"I am not going to pretend I understand."

He is smitten by her honesty, her naiveté, her frankness. "Often a man needs to share a road. Dog shares mine."

"His name is Dog!"

"Yes."

"That's funny. Why is your automobile so clean?"

He scratches the side of his nose trying to bury his need to smile. "It just *is* I guess," he manages to say.

But her expression asks for more. "Well, go ahead."

"Go ahead with what?"

"Guess. No dead insects? No dust? What's your guess?"

He scuffs his boots in the dry soil like a child under the scrutiny of a grandmother. "Maybe insects and dust don't need to collide with a moving 'automobile' if they don't have to."

"And you believe that?"

"No reason colliding with anything if it means not coming back, is there? No reason unless you want to. Or need to."

She drifts away from Dog, the silhouette of her body against the orb in the sky alluring. "But people do," she says.

"Do what?" He finds himself asking.

"Collide."

"Maybe," he answers cautiously.

She looks him in the eye. "If they must, if they need to."

Eyes locked, neither shifting their concentration, neither breaking the rhythm of the dance that they have somehow committed to.

"Who is it you are hunting Just Joe - you and Dog?"

He takes his time in answering. He sees her as she is, cannot sense a ruse or an ulterior motive.

"I am looking for a piece of me," he offers, his voice somewhat soft and wary, cautious of her response.

She looks him over again. There is nothing deliberate about her appraisal. It is open and frank. I am, you are, we could be.

"What is that piece exactly?"

"Let's call it history," he advises.

She nods, and then smiles. "I'm glad we collided, Just Joe. Aren't you?"

"That would depend on your husband, wouldn't it?"

"I don't have a husband!"

"I saw you with a child...?"

"Katherine? Katherine isn't a child. Not a real child. She's a doll. She's my mother's doll. We just pretend sometimes."

"You pretend?" He asks, but he cannot avoid the confusion in his voice. She recognises this and steps closer to him.

"What Sarah, my mother, says the future could be like, will be like. That's what we pretend. Sarah says the more we believe in our dreams, the better the chance of them becoming true. Is she right, or wrong?"

He's aware of her proximity, her smell, her sweetness. "Nothing wrong in believing in something you want. I guess it's about wanting the right thing. I don't know."

"I must go home now, Just Joe," she says with a quick smile.

"I'll give you a lift -- tie your horse to the back...? Drive slowly...?"

She looks at him and then she glances to The Sow. Dog sits contently beside her.

"No," she suddenly says. "I'll race you. Hero and I will race you, you and your automobile."

The Sow on the move and it is kicking up a trail as thick and long as a sand storm.

Out of the dust trail, Danya appears on her horse -- she's bent low over the animal's neck, riding like a trooper, giving the horse rein.

Joe can see her in the rear-view mirror and he grins. He turns up the music in the cabin and he doesn't know why he does.

Truck and horse together -- rider and driver sharing the thrill of speed...and because of the sheen, the colour of The Sow, horse and rider melt with metal, become one. They collide on the move as shifting shapes.

The Sow slows, allowing Danya to come up alongside – Joe and Danya make eye contact...then she spurs her horse forward and she cuts in front of The Sow and the vehicle hesitates, but then accepts the challenge.

She cheats. She leaves the dirt track and heads across country, knowing well the route is untested for any vehicle.

He chuckles, admiring.

The Sow steers toward and under The Monument, partly engulfing the structure with its plume of dust, engulfing history with a glimpse of tomorrow.

Sky is at the merry-go-round assisting, dragging, Mister Simpson onto one of the crimson coloured horses. Nearby, a group of villagers steer the dodgem cars with the energy of a garden snail. Mister Simpson wears a dinner jacket, bowtie and a pair of khaki coloured shorts. He wears sandals on his feet.

"Please, not today Mister Sky. I feel fine -look..." Mister Simpson pulls away from Sky and there and then uses his frail limbs to imitate a jig, the dance of the past. "You see? I danced with Rebecca last night, Mister Sky -- I...we were in step. We laughed together! Mister Sky? We...we kissed -- my wife and I kissed. Mister Sky?"

"What day is it?"

Mister Simpson deflates. "It is Wednesday," he answers with a sigh.

There's a sudden sinister tone in Sky's voice. "Yes, YOUR day, YOUR time. We booked it. Get on that horse now. You cannot change the booking, Mister Simpson. Changing the booking makes Trader very,

very pissed off and you wouldn't like that to happen, would you?"

Dutifully Mister Simpson allows Sky to help him onto the immobile, never blinking effigy of the horse. "No, Mister Sky."

Sky shoves forward a lever and the solar driven carousel, cogs complaining, begins to rotate. "Then off you go."

Sky glances over to the dodgem car track where a driver nudges his car into the rear of another. Sky shakes his head, disillusioned. "That's not how you play the game, Mister Smithers," Sky shouts. "You have to hit him, not kiss his arse!"

He senses someone beside him. He watches Mister Simpson complete the first circuit of the merry-go-round. "I told him what you told me to tell him," he tells the person beside him.

Trader nods. He wears a pale linen suit and small, oval sunglasses. He's conspicuous. "And what was his response?"

"Nothing - he said nothing."

"A Digger is a man of few words, Sky. Good."

Sky turns on Trader."Good? The sonofabitch just looked through me! As if I was a piece of turd -- as if I wasn't there; looked clean through me. How's that good?"

"Because that meant he knows I know." Trader turns on his heels and walks off.

Sky clenches his teeth. He leans forward and thrusts the lever linked to the merry-go-round a further notch forward. Cogs, pinions and music speed up. Mister Simpson grabs onto the horse's neck as the rotating circular platform shifts into canter speed.

"You better hang on there, Mister Simpson. It's your Time, so hang on! Still the gallop to come and after that, who knows..."

In the town of Erasmusville, The Sow turns into the top end of the street like a huge silver tank and slides to a stop. Joe sits back on the driver's chair. He is looking down the street.

Danya has ridden in from the West, the sun behind her. Her horse's flanks shine with sweat. She pats the animal's neck as she watches The Sow. There's a soft smile on her lips.

Joe wills The Sow forward. He focuses on Danya, ignoring the villagers that are stepping out of their houses. The vehicle eases forward. Dog remains mute, his attention forward.

Danya remains poised on her horse.

Reverend Dickinson steps out of his Church, winces against the sudden glare. It takes him a second to read the situation. He catches movement as he notices Sarah exiting her house. They make brief eye contact. The hostility is there, competitive.

Now Danya suddenly spurs her horse forward.

Joe speeds up The Sow.

Like jousting knights of the old, horse and metal head for one another.

Sarah hurries forward toward the garden gate.

The ever surging dust, the horse's feet, the wheels of The Sow. Joe and Danya, their eyes locked. The horse is at full stretch beneath her. Joe sees only her. This is the collision they spoke of. It is imminent. People and structures a blur.

The mirrored sheen of the vehicle's hide reflects the approaching horse and its rider. As they near, the two images merge, become one. It is as if The Sow has swallowed up Danya and her horse. They are entwined in the dust, as if they have become one.

Sarah pales.

The Sow has stopped. Joe sits behind the wheel. Dust is settling. Danya, still mounted on her horse, has stopped not three feet away from the huge bonnet of the whispering vehicle.

In their way, they have collided. They know it and they share it privately. Danya breathes heavily, her horse restless. Joe unclenches his hands from the steering wheel, his eyes never leaving hers.

Sarah watches from her house. She has not moved.

Slowly, Joe gets out of The Sow and Dog shifts on his perch, his eyes hooded.

Reverend Dickinson hesitates on the steps of the Church. He looks across to Sarah. He offers what might be construed as a smile of victory toward her, and then he enters the Church.

Danya dismounts and she watches Joe as she strokes her horse.

The villagers remain mute, their bodies tense with what they have just witnessed.

From across the street, Mister Harry and his two cohorts wearing the uniforms of the Border Patrol, hurry as fast as their ageing limbs can.

Danya and Joe keep their distance.

Sarah turns and enters her house.

"I won," Danya tells Joe.

"I'd say nobody lost. You know where to find me, Danya."

"Yes I do, Just Joe."

Their liaison concreted, Danya takes up the reins and leads her horse away toward the house. There is a muted silence amongst the villagers as they watch Danya lead away her horse, before swinging their attention to Joe.

An elderly woman, her plastic raincoat tight against her body, breaks the silence."You had us a little worried there, young man! It could have been a serious accident."

There's a murmur of consent amongst the gathered and Joe turns to them. He again absorbs their fragility, their age, the manner in which they lean into the endless breeze as if their bodies have now evolved into being a part of it. That they all represent a time long before his, is important to Joe. It deserves respect.

"Maybe you all should have a bit more Faith. Get the Reverend to open that door more often..."

"Oh! He can't do that -- the dust gets in you see," offers the lady in the raincoat.

A man with a slight hunch and wearing a walrus moustache glances at the woman. "I don't think the young man meant it in a realistic sense, my dear."

"Neither did I," she smiles.

Joe spots Mister Harry and his cohorts as they join the gathered crowd, all out of breath and perspiring freely. Mister Harry carries a bolt action rifle, somewhat antiquated.

Mister Murray, adjusting his frayed tie, steps forward and offers his hand as he introduces himself. "Murray, John. Mister Murray." But Joe does not accept the man's hand. He offers a nod of his head instead. There's an awkward pause. "Well, fine show even if I say so myself," Mister Murray offers. "Got my blood boiling which, between you and I, is an occurrence about as rare nowadays as me taking a painless, rapid piss."

Joe is looking at Mister Harry. "How long have you been wearing those uniforms for?" He asks Mister Harry.

But Mister Murray continues his rambling. "It certainly brought back a memory or two! Chicken we used to call it -- I drove a BMW myself. Flash it was and attracted a crowd, especially the ladies. I remember..."

"Will you hush? The young man is trying to ask Mister Harry a question!"

"You were?"Asks Mister Murray before Mister Harry can respond.

"I was asking after the uniforms?"

Mister Harry is about to open his mouth but Mister Murray again beats him to it. "Oh! They go back thirty, twenty-five years. They were enrolled when the migration began -- patrolled on horseback. To keep corporate land safe from the immigrants so the top brass said. 'Grenzschutz!' they were called. Before your time I guess. Damn waste of a taxpayer's money. They were a bloody law unto themselves. Then, of course, they, ah, disappeared."

"Why's that?" Joe asks, but he is now aware of Mister Bob who stands on the porch of the general dealer store. Mister Bob isn't moving, just watching.

"Well -- they went out hunting the wrong man, didn't they?" Mister Murray explains. "David Erasmus was our voice against the Conglomerates ...Border Patrol knew that...a tank of gasoline in the end, Erasmus said, would cost your family a life. Damn right of course...in fact, cost more than one life in the end."

A murmur of consent from the villagers and Joe tries to ignore Mister Bob's appraisal.

"You don't bite the hand that is attempting to protect you, do you? Or hunt the only man that cared a rat's ass about what Mother Nature was feeling? No, Sir."

Joe gestures at Mister Harry who has succumbed to silence. "They died looking for Erasmus?"

"Unfortunately, not ALL of them snuffed it. Four died, but *we all* died a little when they went looking for Erasmus, young man."

"We are *still* dying, Mister Murray..." says a man who wears a cravat.

"Right of course, Mister Chalmers -- but life is what it is...what we make of it."

Joe acknowledges the statement with a nod, a smile. "That I can't deny," he says and steps toward The Sow where the shape of Dog offers sanctuary.

"What a nice, polite young man," the raincoat lady tells the group.

Joe hesitates, keeping his eyes on Mister Bob who acknowledges Joe with a raised hand. "Mind if I ask you why they're wearing the uniforms today?"

"Reverend Dickinson said they should," Mister Murray tells Joe's back as he gets into the Sow. "Not the foggiest idea why," Mister Murray concludes.

Sarah stands in the only window of her lounge and watches The Sow drive past. She wonders, momentarily, why there is no engine sound to the vehicle, a sound she remembers well, of congested traffic and of gaping exhausts. This fleeting lapse is quickly interrupted as she hears Danya's bedroom door close.

Sarah picks up Katherine the doll that has been resting in its nearby crib and calls out. "Danya - Katherine is in here...?"

Silence, so Sarah walks down the corridor carrying Katherine. "Danya?"

Danya sits in her bedroom that is the colour of a lily. Her bed is narrow, its shingle sheet of linen offering respite against the ever needed night's chill.

"I'm a little tired, Mother. I think I'll rest for an hour if that's alright?"

Danya lies down. She draws her knees up against her chest. She is revisiting a moment and she closes her eyes to walk the memory.

Sarah stands in the narrow corridor, cradling the doll that is called Katherine.

"I was frightened for you, Danya. In the street...what were you playing at?" Sarah asks the closed door.

"It was a game. The same as you and father used to play. Remember? As you once told me? In the heat of the moment you described it...isn't that what you said?"

"It doesn't matter what I once said, Danya. You could have been killed!"

"I don't think so, Mother," Danya tells the space of her bedroom.

"It was juvenile. It is too early in any kind of game to be taking those kinds of risks. You could have been hurt. I'll wake you for tea..?"

"That would be nice. Thank you."

Sarah pauses in the corridor. She takes a deep breath. She looks at her hand. It is shaking a little. She composes herself, and heads for the kitchen, cradling Katherine as if the doll was as troubled as she was.

CHAPTER TWELVE

It is night. The moon in its quarter phase teases the dark with a promise of silver shadows.

Joe works on his hands and knees. He has no need for an oil lamp. He works by instinct as he pulls out the final remains of the skeleton, a hint of clothing and what was a leather boot. There is a foot, a spinal bone and a pelvis. He moves the bones about, trying to put them in the place of the past they represented; of the moment they represented.

Dog hisses, his wings outstretched.

Joe sits back on his heels, lights a roll-up in his usual manner, the match a spark in the dark. He studies the skeleton, the glow from his cigarette like an idle glow fly.

"Are you concentrating, Dog?"

Dog swings his head, blinks.

I am Dog and it is marrow I seek.

"Bones they are to you but maybe, just maybe, there is still a life."

Joe crouches beside the skeleton. He puts a hand over the skeletal pelvis but doesn't touch it. His hand hovers, searching.

"I need you here now Dog and to cover my back. It could be a long road I travel and if you don't see my headlights in a few hours...you know what to do. Eat me clean, Dog."

I am Dog. It is not because he fears pain that he bites into the leather, but for the fear of past horrors and being entrapped by them.

In the Trader's oval room the mechanical roof is ajar, inviting the little moonlight to illuminate the anthology of suspended timepieces that, suddenly, shift like a wind chime in a bewildered gust of wind. Their motion is slight, as if being passed over by an invisible wave of energy. Then they go dormant.

Sky leans in the doorway. He is shirtless and drinks an amber liquid from a heavy crystal glass recently inherited from a recently deceased bumper - car victim; heart attack by forced collision the coroner report would have read.

"Digger is at work."

Trader, at his desk, looks up from sorting through a collection of stamp albums, the magnifying glass in his pale hand like a baton.

"Good."

Sky kicks away from the doorframe and saunters into the office. "Like some lost aardvark. Digging away like there's no tomorrow. Why hasn't he come to see you yet?"

"He will."

"It's all bullshit."

"Bullshit?"Trader asks as he sets the magnifying glass aside.

"Yes - all the rumours and the stories about his type are hearsay. Sunday school shit. Why? Were his testicles protected from the sun and nobody else's? What's he got – suntan lotion as sperm? Maybe he can't breed? Maybe, just maybe, he doesn't WANT to fuck. "

"I doubt it."

"You think you know it all? Well, this ball of turf we're sitting on isn't spinning the same anymore in case you forgotten -- no more big, wide and wonderful circles but tiny, hurting little turns with some pretty screwed up people clinging on for survival who will believe in anything. Am I right?"

Trader watches Sky over a steeple of his fingers. "How can I forget, Sky?"

"...no reason why the Digger shouldn't be as everyone else...no reason."

The steeple of fingers collapses. "There is!"

Sky teeters in the middle of the office, his concave, hairless chest pale in the lamp's light.

"Yeah - surprise me?"

Trader flips the pages of the stamp album, peruses history condensed in thumbnail print. "Another time, perhaps," he whispers.

Sky changes tack. He sits on the corner of the desk, touches Trader on the cheek -- now a boy."I just want to know -- so you'll be proud of me...maybe I can be like him?"

Trader takes hold of Sky's hand, holds it against his cheek. "My dear boy -- I don't want you to be like him....even to be a sort of him."

"But you respect the Digger? I know. I can see..."

"Respect - no. Admire, yes. Any man who can still care for purity and love on this tiny, hurting, little planet as you called it deserves admiration," Trader tells Sky as he quickly kisses his finger.

Sky jerks his hand away, stands. "You are in love with him!"

"Don't be ignorant."

Sky gets off the desk, his feet landing hard on the cobbled floor. "You want her to fall in love with him, don't you? You are full of shit, Trader."

Trader remains behind his desk as he listens to Sky's angry footsteps fading away in the gloom of the Church. Then he closes the album and moves to the door of the oval room. He watches his chandelier of timepieces and slowly he mimics a dance. It is the waltz; perhaps the last.

The rising orb of the sun defines The Monument, carves it as a silhouette - it is a dark shape rising from the barren plains, an altar representing the past. The fine sand blows about the base of the structure, weirdly so -- gently spiralling like a devil wind with nowhere to go or to hide.

He is sweating. The muscles of his hands taut, fingers are shaped like talons, suspended without a shudder over the skeleton. He has been in this position for some hours; unmoving and earthed, rooted to the soil that contain the chemicals and spoils of the past.

Poised over the skeletal remains like a vulture, yes, like Dog.

A sudden spasm that begins in his fingers and forks through his entire body and the abrupt, epileptic gyration of his frame is suffice to intrude into Dog's moment of lapsed concentration. The bird raises his body, tensing, now alert.

Joe is connected to the earth, and with the events of many, many yesterdays.

Abruptly he spits out, almost vomits, the leather strip that has now calcified over the hours between his jaws. His eyes glaze over as he searches out his new environment.

"What is he saying?" Joe suddenly shouts. His head rotates on his neck, the iris of his eyes dilating, rolling back into his head. Like a blind man on a highway, Joe rocks on his heels, but his hands, fingers do not budge over the skeleton's pelvis.

"Put. It. Down. Now!" Joe suddenly screams his jugular protruding.

Dog lifts his enormous wings, holds them aloft, the morning light making their grey a blue.

I am Dog. He shares the words of the past. The same words I, and you, have heard before.

Joe swings his head, looking toward the rear of the canyon. But he's not seeing anything in his trance. He is being buffeted by the energy of the dead.

I am Dog. Absorb the negative you become a negative. Fight it and you survive.

Joe is hurled off his haunches and as he flies backwards, he is grabbing for his ears, as if hearing a brutal explosive sound. Like the sound of a Glock pistol, the whine of an incoming bullet.

Dog hisses.

Joe hits the earth hard, rolls, lies there...nothing. Still.

Dog looks down on Joe -- he angles his head, eyes blinking. He jumps off the boulder and waddles over to Joe's body. He puts his beak close to Joe's sweating face. Dog tilts his head.

Then Joe exhales, opens an eye slowly, and looks into Dog's offered eye.

"It's not your time yet, Dog."

Dog blinks.

Joe lies still, his chest heaving under the beginning of the day's heat.

Outside his Church, Reverend Dickinson attempts to sweep away the night's collection of dust on the single step leading up to the door. He works the bristle broom with little enthusiasm, his thoughts and energy pointed toward the Ferguson house across the street. There is a sense of defiance in the Reverend's mood toward the house, or, at least, toward one of its occupants.

In the Ferguson house, Sarah watches Reverend Dickinson through the gap in her lounge window's curtain. She closes it, shuts the man out of her thoughts as she hears Danya enter the room.

"You're awake."

"What were you looking at?"

Sarah fluffs a cushion that has forever lost its fluff. "Not much. Sweet dreams?"

Danya hovers in the doorway. "I think so. Joe..."

"His name is Joe?"

Danya shakes the sleep from her brain."What?"

"You said his name, Danya. Joe. Is that his name?"

"Yes. Just...Joe," she answers, trying to hide her smile.

"Good. I presume after yesterday's game you find him acceptable?" Sarah asks as she sits down on the edge of the small couch that has one leg balanced on a brick.

"I don't understand, mother?"

Sarah pats the couch beside her and she waits for her daughter to sit beside her. Sarah claps her hands together, taps her lips with them before she speaks. "Every since your father joined the migration and selfishly forgot to return to this God forgotten town, I have cared for you and protected you. As it got nastier on the outside, I have done my best to make you feel safe on the inside..."

"I know that."

"Let me conclude. I have wrapped you up within these walls, kept you isolated from what was happening out there; oblivious to the violence, the heat, the diseases, the sorrow and the political lies. I kept you safe in a past I loved -- where there was no ugliness. But now you have met a man; a fine man by the looks of things. So -- I just want to make certain you understand -- I have no reservations whatsoever in you, seeing this man again. That is if you want to. There, I said it!"

Danya keeps looking at her mother. "Why are you crying?" She asks softly.

"Am I?"

Danya reaches up to touch her mother's tears, but Sarah takes a deep breath and stands.

"I'd better fetch a handkerchief..."

Sarah leaves the lounge and walks into the corridor. She steps deep into the corridor to make certain she cannot be seen through the door. From her dress pocket she removes a handkerchief and dabs her eyes.

Her face is a mask as she puts away her handkerchief.

The Sow transports Joe to the cemetery on the fringe of Trader Village. He travels without Dog. Leaving the automobile, Joe takes his time entering beneath the gates. The long coat he wears swirls the dust around his ankles.

Dusk collects over the barren hills, its mantle spreading rapidly.

He sees the gravestones and the crude wooden crosses. In the distance he can hear the inexorable, static tainted music of the merry-go-round. There are no inscriptions on the gravestones. No dates or names. He squats.

What he feels, registers, makes him blink, wince. He stands quickly and walks to the rise of the hill where he can look down on the village. His shoulders are squared, the line of his jaw set. He views the haphazard glow of oil lamps illuminating the street and those that glow weakly from a window or two. In another time, it might have been described as picturesque.

Joe takes the well trodden path toward the village.

Joe stands on the perimeter of the Merry-go-round and the dodgem circuit. He lights a cigarette, recognises that the people are dressed in evening wear; he sees the elderly couple who dance a slow waltz to a dated rock song, their bodies out of synch, like the rhythm of their lives. He absorbs the poignancy of this old love, but shows little emotion even when the woman holds her frail husband's face to her velvet clad bosom.

Joe's eye's barely shift when he senses the man pause beside him.

"You've made dying a business," Joe tells Trader.

"Haven't we both?"

Joe faces Trader, his height dwarfing the man. The rotating image of the carousel is reflected in Trader's spectacles.

"No -- I fill in the holes behind me. You don't and never will. People like these deserve to rest peacefully -- you are killing them before their time. You are leaving holes."

Trader shrugs. "I gather then you visited our cemetery," he says. "But kill is such a harsh word -- I help liberate them. I release them from the shackles of a bleak future. If you dislike what you are seeing, or should I say feeling, why did you come?"

Joe extinguishes his cigarette beneath his boot. "A light needs a dark. That way we know the difference."

"Ah yes - the negative and the positive. Yes, we do need each other," Trader agrees with a soft smile.

"The boy Sky - said you knew about the wall..."

"You aren't surprised that I know?"

Joe doesn't shift his look from Trader's face.

"That was a fatuous question. May I invite you for a drink, to consider a trade?"

Joe follows Trader up the sparsely lit street. He's conscious that the people they pass do not look Trader in his eyes. They are almost subservient in their attitude toward the frail man.

"You may ask the question," Trader tells Joe as they near the Church.

"What question is that?"

"The chicken before the egg question; what came first, this village, or Erasmusville? Answer is Erasmusville," Trader explains, hesitating near the front of the Church. "After the youth migrated, the elderly, the flotsam, got to building Erasmusville. They had managed to salvage some of their possessions. I sniffed a business, gathered a flock of them and here we are."

Joe nods, staring across the street toward the replica of Danya's house. It is dark and shuttered.

"I see nobody's at home?"Joe asks.

Trader's eyes smile behind his spectacles. "No. Not yet. But you may know more about that, than me."

In the damp moonlight, the shapes of Hef, Charles and Sampson snake down the wall of the canyon. They are, strangely, adept at this. Once on the floor of the canyon, they pause, their lungs stretching. Then they proceed. They are all armed with shotguns.

Hef's boots narrowly pass-by the skeleton on the ground, the one Joe discovered.

Joe stands in Trader's study. Oil lamps fuelled with animal fat illuminate the space but the oval room beyond the arch remains inquisitively dark. Trader is unlocking a desk drawer. Joe is uncomfortable in this room. His usual stance of calmness is now one of circumspection; he sees the walls, but not the man.

Joe registers Sky's entrance into the room with a slight glance. "I thought this was between you and me?"He asks Trader.

"Don't mind me, Digger..."

Trader checks Sky from over his shoulder as he works the lock. "Think of him as a fly on the wall," he tells Joe.

Sky roams the room. "That's right – I'm just a fly on the wall. A fly that's been buggering him for the last four years, you know? I'm as hard as rock... able to cleave a clam if you asked me to."

Sky's rehearsed charade hangs heavily in the space. Joe watches Trader for his reaction.

"There was no call for that. Get out," Trader whispers from deep in his throat.

Sky shrugs. "Sorry - thought this was a meeting between men."

They both listen to Sky's receding footsteps.

"I apologise for such vulgarity from such a handsome mouth."

Joe shrugs. "He was talking to you, not me."

"Maybe he was, maybe he was not," Trader responds with a smile as he withdraws an object from the drawer. It is preserved in a glass cubicle – thick glass, magnified and secure.

It is the fob-watch. It is intact, other than for a cracked glass.

"The trade I suggest is sixty-forty in my favour. I show you how to locate Erasmus's rotting debris, you go off and read his history, and we find the diamonds. That's the trade."

Joe doesn't hide his frown. "I'm not here for any diamonds, Trader."

"Don't treat me with ignorance," Trader suddenly barks. His voice is surprisingly strong. Trader takes a breath. "It is common knowledge, historical, that Erasmus took the whereabouts of one of the largest alluvial diamond fields to his grave. You know it and I know it...and any man sourcing that field will not only earn great wealth, but he will bring rejuvenation to this sorrowful, dying landscape. So don't dance the dance with me, Digger. Am I understood?"

"I look for Erasmus. That's all I need to explain."

Trader stares at Joe. Joe doesn't flinch.

"I see," Trader says finally. "For some reason I believe you."

"I am up against a wall. You know that. If these diamonds you speak of are connected to Erasmus in any way, then I will accept your trade. If they are not, you lose."

"And what do you gain?"

"That's personal."

Trader chuckles, his chest wheezing with a whistle."I like a good trade, a good challenge. We have a deal. Here, take this."

Joe accepts glass cubicle.

Trader moves to his desk where he begins to pour two glasses of amber fluid. "That was Erasmus's personal timepiece. It is inscribed, but I found it meaningless."

Trader has his back to Joe as Joe looks at the fob-watch behind the glass. Trader is unaware of the calming of Joe's features, like a man who has discovered a lost belonging, or a man remembering a fond, distant memory.

"'Watch my teeth' is the inscription," Trader recalls from memory as he turns to Joe offering him a glass of the unclear nectar. "It was found in the canyon by a pretend Digger. He had hit the wall. Was demented by the time I purchased it from him. It belonged to Erasmus. It was his pride and joy."

Joe accepts the drink, keeps the container in his hand. Trader studies him, looking for a way to connect but he cannot.

"If you are who I think you are, that instrument should suffice," Trader tells Joe as he walks into the dome. "Like his bones, it was a part of him."

"The last moments of a man's life aren't made of metal, cogs and wheels."

Trader begins operating the mechanical winch within the dome - the suspended timepieces dormant. Joe keeps his distance, listening to the grinding of the gears and cogs as they entwine like the innards of a Victorian flour mill.

"True, but they *are* made of Time, and Time has a memory, a recollection. Time is energy. It has a positive journey - always going forward and collecting information, emotions, and even thoughts...just like ourselves. After all, are we not governed by it?"

Joe steps into the archway, glimpses the suspended timepieces as moon and star light invade the room through the opening in the dome's ceiling.

"This is my collection - my archive. Here survive the dead -- their history continues. A library of the power of collected Time - just waiting to be read, just waiting for the light."

"Then go ahead, light it up," Joe tells Trader.

Trader swings on his heels and confronts Joe. "Don't patronise me!"

Trader tries to recompose himself as he takes the timepiece from Joe's hands and begins to suspend it from a waiting thread."Like most, my thoughts are as polluted as the atmosphere above - as the air we breathe. Unlike you, Digger, the souls that walk the remains of this planet have had their very essence, their inner being, their spirit, corrupted and darkened - the consequences of counter evolution perhaps? Our light has been eternally snuffed out."

Trader stands back, the fob-watch in its glass cubicle attached, hanging. "But your light is bright, Digger. It *shines* eternal. You are fortunate. Some may even say Blessed."

"I follow a road. That is all."

"Yes. Yes I suppose we all do in the end, but yours is chosen, by whom or what I doubt even you can answer."

Trader stands back from the chandelier of Time. He pinches the nerves on the bridge of his nose. "I believe it is all in your hands now. The wall, I think, is separated by seconds...by time, which is an obstinate beast, dangerous if you try to separate it from reality."

Joe hands Trader his empty glass and steps into the dome. Trader watches as Joe removes the leather strip from his coat pocket. He watches as Joe bites down onto it.

Dog, perched near the canvas tent, raises his magnificent, well journeyed wings and hisses in anger at Sampson. The man, his bulk shadowed abnormally in the moonlight, taunts the bird by waving his shotgun and rotating his posterior and gut.

Behind Sampson, Hef and Charles trash Joe's gear like idle youth.

"Shut that fucking bird up," Hef tells Sampson.

"Okay," says Sampson.

And he shoots Dog.

A spray of Dog's blood tattoos Sampson's face.

The sound of the shot echoes.

The barrel of the shotgun exhales a ring of smoke like a lazy cigar smoker.

A feather floats with nowhere to cling.

"You idiot," Hef shouts.

"What? You said shut it up?"

"I didn't mean blow it to rat-shit and feathers!"

"It's dead," says Charles.

"Steal some of this crap and let's get out of here."

I am Dog. I remain as ever. Do not concern yourself. Not yet. Only time will tell.

He caresses the fob watch. He sees that the glass face is cracked and does not remember it as ever being so. The hour hand is on nine, the minute hand stopped short of forty after the hour, dead to further movement, stalled in history.

He cups his right hand over the watch.

Trader cannot participate. He knows that. He can only observe and be privy to what is another man's gift. His feet are transfixed to the floor.

Joe moves his right hand over the watch.

There's a slight shift amongst the suspended timepieces - like tendrils seeking out a hint of sunlight, of life; a sound of metal against metal, tiny and hollow, similar to a bat's wings.

Hef, Charles and Sampson, now perspiring in the night's heat, thread their way between the boulders strewn in the canyon as they approach for the rock face.

"What was that?" Hef asks, pausing in stride.

"I didn't hear anything."

"You never hear anything..."

"Listen," Hef whispers.

It's a faint sound - like pebbles shifting down an embankment.

Now he's caressing a space above the watch. There's a flicker to the minute hand. It moves. Not forward, but backwards.

The suspended timepieces are beginning to mobilize - gyrating, picking up a momentum and energy.

Hef, crouching, moves forward.

"Let's just get out of here!"Charles whispers.

"Shut-up...could be a rabbit. I'm hungry."

Hef moves forward in an awkward, cumbersome crouch, shotgun at the ready.

The suspended timepieces are revolving now - gathering positivity and reason.

The second hand of the fob watch, set in its own little dial, begins to rotate.

Then the first image - murky and faint, snapping across the iris; embedding itself with the velocity of a flashbulb of old.

Four horses, a boulder, dank and sweating. Sunglasses and leather boots that...

The minute hand retards by a fraction.

On the rock a stands a box with a flickering light and in the wide, blue sky a bird flying high. Circling... static and friction, sucked from Hell itself.

He's being bludgeoned by the images and he physically recoils. He staggers as they suck at his life's juices in order to survive, to be. He falters and they fade.

What Trader sees is a man bent over grasping at his innards as if they are tearing him apart. He is no audience, no participant to the images that Joe is experiencing. He will never be.

The minute hand leaps forward by two minutes.

A horse rearing and blood soaks the blade of a Swiss army knife.

The rotating timepieces are slowing. He's on his knees now, looking for support like a man adrift in a storm.

Trader sits on the floor. He does so like a sack of grain. He is weaned of any strength that may have remained in his aged limbs. The rumour of such men, these Diggers, is one thing, but for that rumour to be shredded apart and to show its truth, is another.

Hef, gun at the ready, looks over the curve of the boulder. The sound is sharper now, closer - a rattling sound that is...

It's the bones that Joe left on the ground. They're shifting on the ground -- as if trying to locate the right place of the body to be on...leg bone inching toward thigh bone.

Hef shrieks like an owl that has yet to find his true voice.

He raises his shotgun and keeps pulling the trigger. Shotgun pellets hurl the bones aside in a cloud of dust.

A searing, white light that has...

Joe slow-dancing backwards, his action orchestrated internally, so Trader thinks it is not of this time, this moment of space in time; that it is not human. Joe is breathless, like a marathon runner. He goes to his knees, exhausted, catching his breath; gasping, his mouth bent into an awkward, ghoulish grin by the leather strip he bites on.

Then there is stillness and darkness and the suspended timepieces are suddenly still, like the sand of a beach at low tide, the aftermath of a storm. Just the glow of the night's sky adds realism.

Joe is the first to stand and he does so like a willow in the wind, then he regains his balance, his strength. He removes the leather strip, pockets it.

"What did you experience?"Trader asks, his shrill voice a whisper. He is yet to stand up.

"Not enough...pain and negative."

Trader gets to his feet and he uses the wall to assist him. "That's all?"

"If I tell you more, you'll know more than what we traded for. That would make me redundant."

Trader acknowledges Joe's honesty with a nod. The trade is on; it has been negotiated and Joe has taken the initial step.

Joe, somewhat abruptly, offers his hand to Trader - you have never seen Joe do this before. Trader accepts it, instinctively. As his palm touches that of Joe's, Trader recognises his mistake. Few wish to look in a cracked mirror.

A fear, an uncertainty, crosses Trader's eyes. His already weakened knees buckle slightly. "I should not have done that," he says, ever so quietly.

Joe stares down on Trader, not releasing his grip. "Your father was Nathaniel Trader."

"Yes. What of it?"

Joe does not disengage the handshake. "On the road that I travel I see the consequences of what your father and politicians like him did. You only have to look out that window to know what I mean. No one man, no one town has the right to own and control everything. Not even one country come to think of it. Only adversity and turmoil emerges. He turned the living into bones."

Joe releases Trader's frail hand. He shrugs deeper into his coat as if looking for further armour. "So yes -- to answer what you were thinking, I have seen your father. I am done with you, Trader. I will honour our trade for the diamonds, but beyond that, the agony and suffering that you jail in this room, I have no further interest in. You, Sir, will die by it."

Trader does not move. He massages his hand from the tingle left there. He stands alone, somewhat frail, as the night's light cleaves its way into the dome.

CHAPTER THIRTEEN

In Erasmusville, the blades of a nearby wind pump scissor the moonlight and toss shadows against the rear of the house, camouflaging Danya as she exits the rear door and makes for the shed wall. She clambers over it and disappears from sight.

If Danya had paused to listen she would have heard the Reverend Dickinson's words echoing across the street from the Church.

"Over the years we have prayed for rain and shade, for protection against this infernal heat. We have prayed for those we have lost - we have..."

But she did not pause. Her shape fades into the night.

In the Church, the usual congregation, somewhat irritated - not that there was much else to be doing - to be called at such an hour, watch Reverend Dickinson secure the rear door and as he hurries to a small paper framed window and draw a stained curtain. There's new energy to Dickinson, and some in the congregation are cautiously aware of it.

Reverend Dickinson finally roots himself in front of the pulpit, candles illuminating him.

"We have prayed for sanity to return to those who brought this earth to its present, arid, crippled, drought ridden state. We have prayed for..."

"...copulation," offers Mister Murray.

"For LIFE, Mister Murray...for life, but tonight I wish to pray for love. Yes, the promise of NEW life."

A positive, keen murmur amongst the congregation-- they haven't heard this sermon for some time.

"Yes. Love! Love as you have all witnessed it in our very own street - two people with complete trust and faith in one another."

They did witness the moment and they accept it with a slight shuffling in their hard backed, crude chairs.

"Then why is it a member of this community wishes to spoil that love before it has been given time to blossom? I speak of Sarah Ferguson..."

The congregation shift gear - Dickinson has now added fuel to an already smouldering fire. Could this be the much needed spark?

Shifting shadows in the moonlight. On the edge of the canyon's west wall, Sky moves himself between cooling boulders toward the edge. There he settles, there he is able to see Joe's camp, as well as...

...the headlights of The Sow approaching, damp beams, more orange than silver, illuminating the chaos left behind by Hef, Charles and Sampson.

Sky gravitates to the ground like the worm he is and hides.

The Sow brings Joe to a stop. As the glow from the headlights fade, he computes the damage caused to his camp, the scattered utensils, the ripped canvas of his tent, the upturned stove. The Sow goes still and Joe climbs out of the vehicle.

"Dog? What happened here, my friend? Dog?" He calls into the silver night.

Then he sees Danya -- she is on her knees near the camp and in front of her are the bloody remains of Dog. Red tainted feathers and a head askew.

She looks up at him and her tears sparkle on her cheeks

"Danya...what happened?"

She rocks on her heels a little, her chest heaving and he crouches beside her. He takes a look at Dog before he embraces her so that she is nestled in his shoulder, away from the remains.

"Did you see who did this?"

"I came to see you. But I found...I found this..."

She reflects on the blood on her hands but does so like a person who has nothing else to offer.

He puts out his hand and touches Dog's immobile, dormant head. Does not touch, touch it, just senses it, and hovers over it.

He sees the image he needs to – a shadow, hulking.

She stares at the blood on her hands. It is foreign to her.

"No dream your mother can ever imagine can be as real as that blood...that past...that life. That waste of life." He speaks softly, consoling, not preaching.

With a sullen grunt he stands and walks away. She observes as he finds a shovel. She does not speak as he slams metal into already dead soil. She knows and feels, that this is his time and he must employ it alone, work it out.

Sky, cramped between boulders, can see all he needs too. He can see her; he can see the man working the spade into unforgiving soil. He watches with little emotion, or if there is any, it, perhaps, is swamped by events beyond his comprehension. For the moment that is.

She stands. She approaches Joe. He recognises her, raises the shovel...but she drops to her knees, and she uses her bare, bloody hands to scoop out the soil...frantically so, trying to rid her skin of the stain...she raises her eyes to him and he feels her determination to bury the hurt...so he drops to his knees and they begin to dig together....and their hands touch...again...and again...

It's what they both feel -- working the soil in the night's heat and it is she, Danya who stands, and strips off her shirt, perspiration visible...and then Joe -- a laugh to obliterate the pain...her nipples pert, baring her heart to the moment.

Sky watches -- now suddenly the loneliest person in the world. Like a child, biting back a sob that comes from his stomach. He is witnessing a union; togetherness that...he bites on the need to cry, tucks his knees closer to his stomach.

Joe putting Dog in the hole...her hands alongside, the sheen of his ribs collecting the dust, her breasts caressing his arms as she works alongside, their fullness pale in the moon's light.

Together they feed the soil back into the hole and with a dusty hand he touches her face and tears and she touches his.

They share their first kiss. A nervous laugh replaces the hurt. They embrace; go to the ground as one body.

Sky has wrapped his legs tight against his stomach and he is crying like a baby. Whimpering, he manages to drag himself away from where he hid, from an act he will never be able to indulge in.

As the rising, white sun scatters odd shadows over the silent Merry-go-round...a sun that is suddenly crossed by the flitting images of the black homing pigeons belonging to Trader....

Sky, showing signs of lack of sleep, quietly closes the door to the now empty pigeon coop. He checks the birds circling above, shielding his pale eyes from the sun. Then he makes his way toward Trader's oval residence.

As a unit, the pigeons spiral and fly to the East.

Sky stands looking down at Trader as the man sleeps. He scrutinises Trader, absorbing his age -- perhaps it is his nakedness, or the expression on his face as he sleeps, but there is a loneliness to the man he has not realised before.

Sky turns and leaves.

Trader rolls over onto his back, opens his eyes. He lies motionless, reflecting.

Joe awakes. He is as naked as he was born. He lies on top of Dog's grave and the recently dug earth adheres to his flesh.

"Danya?"

But she is not there. He sits up on his knees. His hands are pressed hard against the soil of Dog's grave.

"Danya!?"

Joe looks down at his hands -- he slowly raises them -- sensing the positive, the energy there. Splinters of earth rise and collect on his palms.

He lowers his hands, allows them to hover on their accord. Further splinters of earth attach themselves to his palms. He is touching Dog.

A calmness sweeps over Joe. In touch with a fond memory and he keeps his hands there. Then a hint of emotion, a kick in his chest, his eyes closed.

His body caked with dust, Joe crouches over the grave, making contact -- and slowly he raises his arms. He holds them aloft, as if they were a pair of wings.

Sarah Ferguson on a mission as she bolts together two windows -- bolts them from opening. She draws the curtains, obscuring the sight of the Church across the street.

She hurries out into the rear garden and to the pigeon coop. There she begins releasing all her white homing birds -- opening the coop, chasing them with gestures and sounds. The birds obey, taking to the air, wings snapping in the early light.

Joe has his arms spread wide, body hunched on its heels, soaring with a friend. You read his journey behind his eyes, in the fluidity of his body, the tensing and relaxing of his muscles.

Danya comes through the small gate, the homing pigeons now soaring high above, getting their bearings. She looks up at them, is about to start forward when Sarah steps from behind the coop:

"Danya. Get into the house, quickly!"

"Why have you let all the birds go, mother?"

Sarah takes her daughter by the elbow. "In the house! Now, please."

Sarah herds her into the kitchen, slamming the door and beginning to bolt it.

Danya is confused, a little scared. "What is going on?"

"We need to start packing a few clothes. Nothing much..."

"You are not answering me!"

Sarah, the door now bolted, takes a deep breath and calms. "The right, honourable Reverend is calling the people together -- he is mustering the senile Calvary..."

"Why?"

"...he's going to use them to persuade you from seeing Joe...parade the spiritually crippled as some kind of sordid example of what the consequences of illicit copulation are." Sarah looks hard at Danya, unwavering. "Or, in your case, were..."

Danya meets her mother's attitude head-on. "I have done nothing wrong."

Sarah hurries up the narrow passageway, Danya forced to follow.

"He considers your relationship as being blasphemous, Danya." Sarah says as she hurries along. "He considers it an insult against the Church. I anticipated this. Nothing ever changes when it comes down to the Reverends of this world...nothing!"

Sarah looks into the confines of a wall cupboard that treasures a few blankets and a travel bag.

"But I have! I have changed. I need to talk with you."

Sarah removes the large travel bag. "We do not have time for that. Start packing your clothes."

Danya takes the bag, sensing her mother's unreasonableness.

The flock of Sarah's homing pigeons in the air -- crossing the hot sky -- flying to the West...

...as, navigating the same path, Trader's flock of darkly coloured birds fly to the East; opposite directions, but for the same purpose.

The dark is crossing the light.

The brief, flickering shadows cross over Joe. Down there, hunched on his haunches, arms aloft as he rides Dog's thermal, cherishes the freedom and the breeze.

He's perspiring heavily. His weight maybe attached to the earth, but his spirit is elsewhere. He does not hear Reverend Dickinson's words.

"Young man? It is me, Reverend Dickinson. Young man?"

His eyes flutter beneath his eyelids.

The intrusive voice is louder now. "Hello!"

Joe's eyes open. The muscles in his arms remain rigid. The trance eases away from head to foot and then as Joe senses reality, his spins like a feral child, dropping his arms, eyes focusing on the people that have gathered around him.

Reverend Dickinson stands here...and Mister Murray, Mister Bob, the three elderly uniformed Border Patrol, an Elderly Woman, Harry and the Midwife and behind them, others from Erasmusville...grouped and dusty. Some carry personal belongings, water, cans of food and others shovels and crudely adapted pick-axes.

Perched in a wheelbarrow, an empty coffin made from assorted planks forms a macabre sculpture.

"What do you all want?" Joe asks softly, his throat dry." He gestures at Reverend Dickinson, whose cassock is grey with travel. "And you?"

"We have come to help. All of us have and to speak with you."

Joe remains crouched and, as of yet, seems ignorant to his own nakedness. "Where is Danya? Did you see her?"

Mister Murray steps forward, adjusting his tie. "We did. She was riding home."

"We must warn you," Reverend Dickinson says, "that Sarah Ferguson does not want you to see her daughter..."

But Joe is staring in the region of his bare feet; at the ground, where Dog died, where he and Danya made love.

"Do...do you need some water, young man? I...I think he's ill, Reverend?"

"I'll take care of this, Katherine."

"We are here to help..."

He's staring at the dusty, infertile soil. A hint of Dog's blood, a feather...

"...to bury the past that you seek," Reverend Dickinson continues, his voice permeating in waves over Joe. "We want you to love Danya and to cherish her. God knows we want this. Can you hear me?"

He's floating his hand over the soil -- caressing it...as if it were Danya's body, as if he feels the new life that began, that will begin there.

Mister Murray raises his voice to baritone. "Look here -- senile, deaf, half blind and often excreting uncontrollably in our own pants we may all be, but what we witnessed...you and Danya in the street, has invigorated us, young man!"

"Will you please shut up, Mister Murray," Reverend Dickson tells the man.

But Joe is not with these people yet. He continues watching his hand and that patch of soil. There is silence now amongst the gathered villagers; a desperate, curious silence. Joe becomes aware of this and he finally lifts his head.

"It could have been all very simple, you know," he tells them all.

Mister Harry, the store keeper, shifts on his feet. "I...we...think we know who you are?"

The hand has not moved. Not even an inch off the ground.

"Mister Harry believes you are the son of David Erasmus?"The Reverend asks, cautiously.

Joe looks at the Reverend, senses the scepticism behind the priest's spectacles.

"I cannot be the son of an incomplete man, Reverend. You should know that."

Reverend Dickinson manages a quick, nervous smile.

Now Joe clenches his hand into a fist. It is over.

He moves his hand away and there, in the dry soil, a hint of a brilliant shoot of young grass; brilliant in the grey dust.

There is no verbal reaction from the gathered; just a muted intake of dank, hot air.

Joe stands. "All we had to do was listen when we should have...listened to ourselves and to our hearts."

With that said, Joe, stark naked, walks toward The Sow.

"Where...where are you going?" Reverend Dickinson calls out.

"To find Danya - to find my heart," Joe responds, not turning.

"We came to find David Erasmus and to bury him?"Mister Murray calls out. "To make your journey complete...isn't that what you want?"

Now Joe turns and faces these fragile people. "He remains hidden."

"Then we will find him for you," Mister Harry calls out.

"Young man," the Midwife bellows like a foghorn in the mist.

"Yes," replies Joe.

"You can't go to Danya dressed like that, surely?"

Joe looks down at himself. He lifts his head. "No...No Ma'am, I cannot. Thank you."

Reverend Dickinson looks down at the fresh shoot of grass that peeks at his worn shoes and he reins in his need to get down on his knees, either to pray, or simply to sniff the freshness.

CHAPTER FOURTEEN

Trader sits behind his desk; the only shadow in the room is the one that lurks over the lenses of his spectacles. He studies his fingernails. This done to his satisfaction, he opens the drawer in his desk and removes the box that contains Erasmus's timepiece.

That did contain the timepiece.

The glass is smashed. It is empty. He puts the cubicle away in the drawer, closes it, and then rests his hands on the desk.

Thus, he sits.

Out on the plateau, the dust trail hugs the rear end of the horse drawn buggy as a dog does a bitch in heat. Sarah steers the bruising contraption and Danya sits beside her, the hold-all between them.

Though Danya is conscious of Katherine, the doll, she holds in her lap, her attention is on her hands; those hands once stained with Dog's blood, once alive with the touch of Joe.

Then, suddenly, Danya hurls the blinking doll out of the buggy. It spirals in the air, limbs flailing, pirouetting in the sun's rays.

"What are you doing, Danya?" Sarah shouts over the noise of the travelling buggy.

"It's NOT real. Nothing is real. Joe, he showed me...the blood and the feathers. On my hands with the feathers and I realized then that...about breathing and life and when I looked at Joe he knew already what I was feeling so I..."

In the distance, a stationary horse and enclosed carriage pockmark the wasted land. There is no driver, no occupant visible.

"Shut up...Just shut up! I will hear nothing more, Danya. Do you understand?"

"I want Joe."

Sarah steers her buggy closer to the waiting carriage where another, tethered horse turns a disinterested eye toward them.

"I think you have had your fair share of our Mister Joe, Danya. Now say nothing."

Danya grits her teeth. The buggy lurches to a halt and Sarah applies the footbrake before she disembarks and makes her way to the isolated, enclosed carriage. Horses neigh not in greeting, but with tired instinct.

Sarah opens the door, the ill fitted replica brass handle fragile in her hand.

Sky pokes his head out; the imitation velvet of the carriage's upholstery is a blood red and it adds sheen to Sky's white linen suit.

"Hello, Sarah."

"Where is Trader?" Sarah is quick to ask.

Danya senses the hostility in her mother's voice. Something is amiss. She turns away from Sky's prying eyes.

"He has so much to do, in so little time."

"He sent me a message. Why isn't he here?"

"I sent the pigeons, Mrs Ferguson. I sent the little black, fluttering Devils."

"My trade was with Trader, not you, you little, inconspicuous brat."

Sky nimbly jumps out of the carriage and Sarah is forced to step aside. "Inconspicuous? Maybe -- but not for long...where are you going?"

Sarah is stepping back from the carriage and making back to her buggy. "I am taking my daughter home."

"No. Not today or any other day," he says to her back, but his eyes always on Danya.

"I beg your pardon?"

Sky shrugs. "You can go home. But Danya cannot."

Danya is nervous now, even scared. She senses her mother's tension, her defiance toward Sky who, in Danya's eyes, seems small and fragile, like an asp.

Sarah suddenly turns to her daughter. "Danya...ride!" She shouts.

Sky jabs his fingers in his mouth and whistles, the sound sharp in the silence of the plateau.

Danya grabs for the reins as, from behind a cluster of statuesque boulders, Hef appears on horseback. He rides with the butt of his gun against his thigh, his toothless mouth agape with adrenalin.

"Hef - stop her."

Hef urges his horse forward, circling Danya who is now distraught. He dismounts quickly, grabbing at her horse's reins, jerking down on the horse's mouth.

"Don't you touch her you bastard," Sarah warns Hef.

Sky chuckles behind Sarah. "No -- I am the bastard, Mrs. Ferguson...in all its true meaning." He glances at Hef. "Get her off the buggy..."

Sky presents himself to Sarah, solid in his position for one so frail. "Trading your pregnant daughter to share in the wealth, the bounty of the dead may not rest well with Reverend Dickinson and his people."

Sarah's face remains a mask, the stench of blackmail not even teasing her guilt.

"If they got to know," Sky continues, "they'd probably burn you at the stake...I wouldn't put it past them."

"Mother? What is he saying? Is this true? Mother?"

Danya is suddenly grabbed and dragged off the buggy by Hef. She manages to swing her hands and connect with the back of Hef's head, but all the man does is grin in response. Her pins her arms to her side and leers into her neck.

"Danya -- this wasn't meant to happen. I promise you."

Danya's breath is heavy. "You lied to me. You lied to Reverend Dickinson...to yourself! Why? Let go of me you filthy shit."

Sky, with a little rehearsed swagger, puts himself in front of Danya. He drops the tone of his voice. "Your mother -- she sold you out...I get you and the child, she gets to share Trader's wealth. All that antiquated stuff from the past, and, more importantly, the diamonds the Digger will find. History, antiques, I have no interest in. But you...you are the future, Danya. You carry it. Right there," he tells her, and gently nudges her stomach. Hef giggles.

Sarah fights to gain her breath. "He's lying. I'm making sure we have a future, Danya. That you have a proper future."

Danya's glare cripples her mother. Not of anger, more of pity.

Sky senses the mood between mother and daughter and claims it as his own. "Get her into the carriage," he tells Hef pointing at Danya. "And be careful." He glances at Sarah. "Bye, bye, Mother-in-Law. Love to Trader for me..."

Danya is led into the carriage by Hef. She is weaned of any strength by the recent events to fight back; she feels as if she has been dunked in an abyss with her arms tied to her sides.

She does not look back at her mother.

Trader exits the dome near the pigeon coop, Sarah's pigeon's in there, white and pristine.

He smiles condescendingly. Then he becomes aware of a handful of villagers gathered nearby, awkward in their postures, embarrassed almost. Mister Witherspoon stands slightly ahead of the group.

Trader sees that some of the assembled carry possessions; an old suitcase, another with wrapped linen and canvas.

"Leaving town, Mister Witherspoon?" Trader asks, keeping his distance.

Mister Witherspoon stares at his shoes, averting his eyes.

"I understand," Trader says. "There's a promise of a new time...the Digger and the girl...perhaps a future. That would be a fine thing, would it not Mister Witherspoon? Not being dependent on *old* time anymore...not having those minutes eat away our flesh and breath."

Mister Witherspoon lifts his head, relieved. The group of villagers behind him relax their stances. "You'll tell Mister Sky then...that we left?"Mister Witherspoon asks.

"I'm more than certain he already knows," Trader replies. He turns around and returns to the door in the dome as Sarah's pale pigeons settle in their new abode.

CHAPTER FIFTEEN

Salvaged wind generators and the crooked, rotating blades of wind pumps greet The Sow as it transports Joe down the street in Erasmusville.

The midday sun is flat and ferocious. The few villagers that remain keep under whatever shade they can find. They stand glued to their spots like toy soldiers, basking in the half-light.

Joe climbs out of The Sow, the weary dust trail settling immediately like a tired mongrel. Joe makes for the crooked gate.

"Danya?"

His voice rings loud in the sullen silence of the village. "Danya...It's me."

Charles appears from a corner of the house, his shotgun levelled at Joe's stomach. "Hiiiiii," he teases, managing to curl his lips. "It's me," he adds, offering an exaggerated, womanly wave.

"So I see," responds Joe. He hasn't looked Charles in the eyes. Not yet.

"I'm going to shoot your balls off," Charles informs him.

Joe takes out his cigarette case. "No you're not."

Charles giggles and sniffs. "I am, too."

"Is Danya here?"

"You'll never know."

Joe now looks at Charles as he pulls a match from his coat pocket.

"Don't look at me. Okay? I'm going to shoot your balls off...I SAID DON'T LOOK AT ME!"

"I'm not looking. Not really. Not yet."

Then Joe lights the match, passing his hand over it, as he always does. The match flares. He lights his cigarette.

Charles has witnessed this. He is silent. "Holy crap," he finally whispers.

"Is Danya in the house?"

Charles wipes his nose, and then nods, a little too eagerly.

Joe cautiously opens the door.

Sampson stands in the hallway, his shotgun aimed at Joe. The big man grins, his hearing aid prominent.

"You killed Dog," Joe tells Sampson.

"I did what?"

Charles has moved behind Joe where he can see Sampson in the hallway.

"Shoot him. Go on. Shoot him," Charles tells Sampson.

Sampson cocks his head. "What you say?"

"I said shoot him," Charles yells.

Joe hasn't shifted his position in the doorway. He exudes calmness. "You killed dog. You did. I know. Why?"

Joe is staring at Sampson now and already Sampson is wavering; his facial expression taking on the pallor of a man sick at sea.

"Just who or what the shit is Dog?" Charles asks.

Joe stares at Sampson, boring into him. "Dog was the bird, my bird."

"What you gonna do, Sampson? Huh? Huh?" Charles asks Sampson, loudly.

"I don't know...what you going to do? He's looking at me again, Charles."

Joe hasn't flinched.

"Hef - Hef he said to kill the bird. To make it go quiet," Sampson finally admits, incapable of breathing regularly now.

"People like you started the senseless rot and the violence. People like you who should have cared."

"I can't hear you?"

Charles is dancing on his feet with nervousness. He knows it has all gone horribly wrong, that both he and Sampson are sinking in the quicksand Joe has managed to plant.

"I asked you where is Danya?"

"He lit a match! Oh shit...with his hand!" Charles sniffs from behind Joe, his eyes darting left and right.

"Where is she?" Joe again asks, this time louder, but still in control.

"Sky took her."

"Took her where?"

"He said we were to meet at the canyon at sunrise...afterwards."

"Afterwards...?"

Sampson fiddles with his hearing-aid: anything to avoid Joe's presence. "After...after us...Charles, not me...was going to make it so's you...you know..."

"No I don't know..."

"Don't tell him anything Sampson," Charles yells from the background, his boots stirring the dust.

Sampson eyes the floor. "So's you can't breed no more," e tells Joe.

Joe steps closer to Sampson very quickly. "You killed my friend," he says on the move, and then he slaps Sampson's ear, the one without the hearing-aid. He slaps it with a full hand, palm in, and the blow rings out like a pistol shot.

And as Sampson yelps like a struck puppy, Joe is already striding off, past Charles and toward The Sow. Charles dodges out of Joe's path, his feet numb with nervousness, and the shotgun as useless as the sudden air in his bowels.

Sampson, clasping his head, staggers out of the house.

"Sky is going to kill us...Sky is going to take our balls," Charles whispers as he watches The Sow transport Joe away, not even wanting to question or deliberate the silence of the automobile.

"Screw, Sky..."says Sampson.

Charles looks at his friend. "What did you say?"

"I said screw Sky, why?"

Before The Event, the breaking of dawn was a slow unveiling, like a chameleon changing colour, a chrysalis to butterfly – a slow realisation that day was impending.

This is the pace, the crawl, that realisation spreads across Sampson's face. He pulls his hearing-aid away from his ear. He looks at it. He looks at Charles.

"Charles," Sampson says quietly. "I can hear. He's made it so I can hear."

The coming dusk adds a hue to the house that is tucked between two stagnant fingers of rock. The structure is the replica of the Fergusons' house. Even down to the cacti and the rockery. The horse and closed carriage stand outside the building. Hef leans against the carriage, his gun visible, and glares at the coming night as if it were an enemy.

"Not even Trader knows of this house," Sky had told Danya as he had led her toward its entrance. "And those that built it are well on their way to Hell."

A lamp is lit inside the house, adding a one - eye glow to its shape.

Inside the house, Sky blows out the match and lifts up the lamp. It casts it glow over Danya who keeps her distance. They are both in the kitchen, utensils and colour exact.

"Every time my smelly friends went a-visiting you, they'd tell me about the décor," Sky tells her. "It's also exactly the way Sarah described it to Trader. Just he didn't know I was listening. This is all for you. For us..."

Sky bolts the kitchen door and Danya flinches with the action and sound. He steers her down the narrow passageway. "The same prints - took me months to find them, to trade for them, to duplicate. A bit ghoulish I know, but it seems the dying all collect the same."

They enter the lounge, Danya, feeling awash, afloat with the absurdity of this and past events, hesitates. Sky notices this and he takes her by the elbows, turns her so she must see and digest.

"I want nothing to change for you. This is your new home, but it is your old home."

"This will never be my home."

Sky slaps Danya across the cheek. For his slight frame, the blow carries potency and Danya recoils, smarting, but she finds her own strength quickly and she rights herself, glares at him.

"It will be our home. And when our child is born people will come and visit, you see? Guided by a little star, perhaps? That's a joke, Danya! But it will be the ONLY child. In the land of the dead, a child will be King! I thought of that. I did. Really I did."

"What child? What are you talking about?"

"I saw it all, Danya. You and the Digger... I was there...for the conception. It is written. There will be a child."

Danya attacks Sky – she claws at him, her raised knee glancing off his thin thigh. He is as tough as a whippet, defending his body like a boxer.

"I'll kill you!"

"No you won't. I waited too long for this...too long of watching old people die and people looking at me like I'm a nothing. Stop it! Listen to me -- I'm a man just like any of them and I will prove it..."

He has her up against the wall finally, his warm breath coming in grasps almost in unison with her.

She glares at him. "Joe will kill you," she gasps.

"Doubt it... those turd - for- brain friends of mine should be shot gunning his testicles to shreds by now. His sperm may be fertile, but not anymore. Come!"

He drags her down the corridor by the hand and she limps after him. He pauses in front of a door, the door to her bedroom back in Erasmusville, where she last dreamt of Joe and remembered his tones.

"Look."

She shakes her head, tired for words.

Sky opens the door.

Danya does. She must, she has no option. The room is painted blue. It is a fully furnished nursery, its antiquated crib, the floral curtains and the mural of a badly sketched fairy all drawn from the past, rescued and bribed from the dead.

"Blue. I didn't have colours when I was a child. I don't remember any. Do you? Maybe bastards aren't allowed a colour? That's why I chose blue. So he'll know he's not a bastard. What you think?"

She puts her hand against the wall and flinches, for it is the same texture of her home that she has just left behind.

CHAPTER SIXTEEN

It is night when The Sow delivers Joe to the mouth of the canyon; a brooding night speckled by unreachable stars; a brooding dark with a secret locked in a drawer.

Joe sits in The Sow's cabin as its headlights fade. He tries to disregard the faces of the villagers that he knows watch him from the darkness. The emptiness of the passenger seat, Dog's seat, does not evade him. He acknowledges it with a glance. From the window he has seen the sporadic lights offered by the lamps of the villagers. They blotch the canyon floor. A fire or two burn near Joe's camp; the aroma of roasting rabbit reaches him. He tastes his own hunger.

Joe climbs out of the automobile.

"We were concerned you may not return." Reverend Dickinson is the first to speak, white collar like a halo in the dark.

"Where is Danya?" The Midwife asks her voice distant, near the cooking area.

Joe inhales the night's coolness and is thankful for it. "I am told she will be brought here at dawn," he tells the shadowed figures. "There is no reason for any of you to be here. I told you this before. I can deal with Trader."

Mister Murray steps forward. Joe can see that the man is beyond tired, his tweed jacket white with dust. "If you say there is no reason to be here, please give us all a reason to be somewhere else, young man?"

"Why are they bringing her to here at dawn?"

"Who are they - that vile tribe of youth?"

"For God's Sake, let the man speak," orders Reverend Dickinson, his voice sounding strong, no longer pulpit bound, no longer restricted between four, crumbling walls.

Joe, weary, puts his hands deep into his coat pockets. "They told me there is a trade for her. That is all I know. I decided it best to be here than search aimlessly."

In the dark Joe senses the shift of heads in appreciation.

"I think we found something that can help you," offers Mister Bob, the storekeeper. "Not much I know...but maybe a-something."

They stand grouped to the rear of the canyon, near the rock shaped like an over-sized walnut. The lamps they hold burn their animal fat with farts and splutters.

"You have dug deep, very deep," Joe tells them with admiration.

"We concluded," says Mister Murray, "that if a man, as David Erasmus was, was being chased, being harassed, he'd be far safer with his back against a wall."

"Hence we dug here...nowhere else to go."

"And this is what we found."

The coffin on its barrow is parked nearby, waiting like a punctuation mark to be used. A nearby lamp casts its flicker over its wooden hue.

"Is it what you need?" Reverend Dickinson asks. "I...we...were hoping that if what we have found...completes your search, you may stay with us for awhile...you and Danya?"

Joe stares down at the skull; the few vertebrae attached slinking into unspoilt earth like an earthworm; more to be dug, to be revealed. The hole is some four feet deep, narrow, almost a grave for a child.

A lamp extinguishes, its fuel depleted.

"You asking me or setting me up for a trade?" Joe asks the Reverend without shifting his eyes.

"I don't think this is the time," says Mister Bob, "to be discussing this."

"I agree," adds Mister Murray. "We came here to complete the young man's search. It is what we discussed, Reverend...one step at a time, as we used to say."

Reverend Dickinson lifts his pale palms in the night, backing off.

"We think it is David," a voice says.

Mister Harry, the storekeeper steps forward, his feet balanced on the edge of the pit. He looks Joe in the eye without uncertainty. "I know this belonged to him. When we found it, we kept digging."

"We scratched like demented fowl," Mister Murray adds.

Joe looks at Mister Harry. He must. "I am yet to prove that I am David Erasmus's son. In your eyes I may look like him...but there are spaces still unfilled..."

Mister Harry hands Joe the Swiss army knife. Its protruding blade has lost its shine, the once red handle now a pale pink, flecked with age and rust.

Joe takes it in his hand. "Something happened here, something not in real time," Joe tells the gathered crowd.

"There was an explosion," a voice offers.

"A light..."

"...was seen for miles around we remember..."

"...like the beginning of the end."

Joe shakes his head. "No. Not that. It's un-lived time. It's a wall...a space, a gap. That's a dangerous place to travel because it is unknown." Joe squats at the edge of the hole, his audience attentive. "A man's death is immediate. He may suffer, has to wait, but when it happens it is swift. The light is switched off.

He leaves no gap between being and being dead. But here, it is different. The gap waits to be filled..."

Reverend Dickinson clears his throat. "Filled by what?"

"By another life...one will feed the other. It is a space in time."

Joe's words hang heavy.

"If there is doubt and danger, perhaps it should be left alone?" Reverend Dickinson suggests and there is a murmur of agreement from amongst the villagers.

"I need space. And time," Joe tells them, his attention on the skull.

Obediently, the villagers ushered by Reverend Dickinson drift away, their oil lamps bobbing in the dark like buoys on a black sea.

Joe is left alone with the remains of his father.

Trader rests but does not sleep. The new silence of his deserted village blankets him. He is calmed by it, thinks of it as the quiet before the storm. He hears the gentle chime of his timepieces and he leaves his bed and enters the darkness of the dome.

Sarah Ferguson, the light of a candle, paces the kitchen like an actor reciting his lines. She has not slept. She cannot. Katherine, the doll, lies on the table. The figurine has lost a limb and one eye remains unblinking.

In the canyon all, but one, have fallen asleep. Men and woman, wrapped against the night's chill, sleep against boulders, some even beneath The Sow. Reverend Dickinson remains awake. From where he is seated, huddled, he can watch Joe; he can see the man, illuminated by sputtering oil lamps, poised like a talon, like the head of a cobra about to strike. He has been like this for hours now. Unmoving, a model for Rodin he thinks. The power in a hand...does any of this make God Sense? He seeks out the dead to promote the future, to enable it, to re-fuel it. Reverend Dickinson feels his eyes close, and he stirs them awake with the optimistic thought of love and a new born. Like a shoot of green grass. How did he do that? If it was the Devil's work, then good for you Satan. He feels the need for sleep and a drink of the amber fluid. I'm participating in the awakening of the dead to heal your mistakes...tell that from my crippled pulpit I'd be crucified. Sleep...how does he not sleep? And the bird...what happened to the bird? Sleep engulfs.

...as timepieces rattle their history in Trader's dome.

...as dawn sketches a shepherd's warning...is flaming orange.

...the echo of Joe's voice wakes the sleeping, the huddled, interrupts the dreams of the past.

"IT IS ONLY TIME!" Joe's voice, the echo of it, is guttural; disembodied, mimicking the timbre of

Erasmus's voice heard by the same canyon walls so many years before.

Reverend Dickinson awakes in time to see Joe clasp his ears and fall backwards. He struggles to his feet and hurries toward the rear of the canyon to Joe. Others are doing the same.

Sarah urges the horse pulling the buggy on. She is riding to the West, toward the Trader's village. She ignores the scattered trail of people that are approaching her. Mister Witherspoon leads the migration; men and women wearing ball gowns and dinner suits, some clasping suitcases, others each other. They scramble off the dirt track as Sarah's buggy cleaves its way through them. Her face is marble.

Joe is curled on the ground, in pain, breathless...

Reverend Dickinson and the villagers gather around him, but keep their distance.

"It's no use. Some places we're meant to go, some we are not...shut me out again," Joe finally says as he manages to sit up.

"Then best you leave him be," the Reverend says. "Some water perhaps, Mister Murray?"

Joe gets to his feet, finds a boulder to lean against. "The gap is too wide," he tells them. He takes the flask Mister Murray offers him and drinks from it.

"Chin up, young man -- at least we can bury the man with some dignity. Just the day for it -- buried the day he died," Mister Murray says.

Joe straightens. "Erasmus died today?"

"Twenty years ago - March fifteen...is it important for you?"

"What's the time?" Joe asks, his voice a whisper, his mind racing ahead of his vocal chords. "What is the time?"He asks again, impatient and loud.

"Just after seven, Digger..."

Sky's voice infiltrates the canyon from above, its shrillness earning the echo of a whistle.

Joe spots him now, as do the villagers. He's up on the canyon wall, on the edge. Danya is with him, her arms wrapped tightly around her body. Hef is there, toting his shotgun with bravado, pointing it between Danya's shoulder blades. Joe knows Hef is dangerously dumb. He has seen into the man, tested his energy and knows that it is a negative.

"Maybe this will help, Digger," Sky calls out and shows that he is holding Erasmus's fob-watch. "Let's you and I talk."

CHAPTER SEVENTEEN

In his bedroom, Trader completes dressing. He adjusts the cuffs of his shirt, the lapels of his black suit jacket. He is quiet calm. He flicks away a speck of dust from his shoulder. He is dressed as if he were about to attend a funeral.

"You'll like this suit, Father. It was one of your own. I trust you'll find Sky amicable when we meet," Trader tells the morning light in the room. He spins on his heels when he hears Sarah shouting in the street. Her voice is strong with panic.

"Danya...where are you? Danya, please."

Trader hurries into his office and looks through the small window. He sees Sarah clambering out of the buggy, the horse lathered, fatigued. She makes her way toward the replica of her house and out of Trader's view.

Trader leaves the room and makes his way through into the dank Church. He bolts the front door efficiently.

Sky, Danya and Hef have made their way down onto the floor of the canyon. Joe keeps his eyes on Danya and as she nears him, she manages a small, quick smile. The villagers and Reverend Dickinson hover, keeping their distance, uncertain and wary.

"I figured it wouldn't be that simple -- otherwise Trader would have dug this place up years ago. He wouldn't have hung onto this timepiece the way he did unless it meant something important," Sky tells Joe, ignoring the crowd.

"Danya, are you alright?"

"Yes."

Sky applauds softly. "How sweet they are. It's time to trade, Digger."

"Trader knows about this?"

"I'm the man now. It's a simple trade, Digger -- this timepiece or Danya? It's me in control now - Trader is sitting in the dark...like always. Question of money or love, am I right? You know what I mean, Digger. Some of your magic...the mumbo-jumbo...and you can take the wealth. But Danya stays with me."

Mister Murray leans closer to Mister Harry. "Is the kid dumb? Of course our man will take the girl," he whispers.

But Mister Harry looks uncertain.

"If Danya comes with me, you have nothing."

Sky shrugs. "That's my gamble. But I don't think you'll do that. There's unfinished business here for you, whatever it is. Business of a personal nature and you'd never live it down if you walked away. It'll eat away at you like that dumb bird of yours used to eat a carcass."

Danya lifts her head, focuses on Joe; the blood of Dog, a feather in the breeze.

Joe looks at Hef. "Did he tell you to kill Dog?" He asks, referring to Sky with a nod.

"Who's Dog?" Hef asks.

"His ugly bird, you idiot," Sky says. "It was all my doing, Digger. Stimulate you a bit; get the juices flowing. Which it did, didn't it? Now let's get on with this -- time, as they say, is ticking."

Reverend Dickinson steps forward, his spectacles coated in dust. "It is not always about wealth, young man. Look at those about you," he tells Joe, managing to ignore Sky. Joe remains mute, keeps his eyes on Sky.

Sky again shows the timepiece. "Nine forty it stopped. That's sixty minutes away, Digger," he tells Joe. "Trader said it will take a man with courage -- courage to become a part of a man's history, a part of a man's dying? Sharing his final time? Spooky mumbo-jumbo...could suck you in like quicksand is what Trader once told me."

Danya senses the danger now. "Please don't do this, Just Joe," she says, her voice reminding Joe of her presence. He shifts his look momentarily, sees the honest concern in her face.

"Okay enough, now. Let's trade, Digger," Sky says impatiently.

They all watch Joe now, the day's heat already bringing perspiration and a lazy devil wind rises in the distance. Mister Murray tugs his tie and Danya shivers against a chill that has risen from her feet.

Joe steps closer to Sky. "Give me the time-piece," he tells him.

The woman wearing a raincoat quickly smothers her mouth with her dirty hands, drowning out the sound of shock.

Sky grins. "I've never misjudged a character...money speaks. The deal is done, Digger."

"You can't do this! Look at her, man! Think..."Reverend Dickinson shouts his voice suddenly strong.

Joe does look at Danya, the fob-watch now in his hand. "Some people are meant to collide and some just aren't," he tells her and he sees that she recognises his words, and she frowns. "Just the way it is. I'm sorry," he concludes.

Reverend Dickinson stumbles forward. "I implore you! Look into your heart, look deep, look..."

Joe suddenly turns – his stance is aggressive, his back straight as he confronts the priest. "Step away, priest...all of you, step away. What lies here is mine from now on. Now go! Clear these places now...leave the canyon. Leave me! Leave! I am not much your future than you are of your own."

Reverend Dickinson tries to hold his position, but Joe towers over him. "I said get these people away from here, priest," Joe tells him. "As far away as you can."

They begin to withdraw, confused and hurt, fragile in the heat, fragile with the sense of loss. Reverend Dickinson stumbles after them, Joe's warning ringing in his ears, deciphering the tone, the threat, or a message.

Joe turns on Danya. "You're his, not mine," he tells her. "Take her away, far away," he tells Sky.

Sky is thrilled. He's in control and he rubs his pale hands together as if they are charged with electricity and buzz. He glares at Hef. "You heard the man," he tells Hef. "Take her away with the rest of them. The man's got some work to do."

Hef grabs Danya, begins pushing her toward the mouth of the canyon. She manages to throw a look back at Joe, an imploring look, but Joe manages to ignore it.

Joe turns to Sky. "Are you going to stay here with me?"

"I won't interfere I promise."

"No problem," Joe responds.

"I knew we travelled the same road," Sky says watching Joe as he heads toward the base of the rock shaped like an acorn. "Trader is out of touch. I always figured it was the money. All the rest was just poetry and mumbling...heavy stuff with no future."

Joe hesitates near the base of the rock, where Erasmus's carcass rests. Casually, he puts his foot against the coffin there, and pushes it onto its side. The lid of the coffin topples to the ground. He then climbs the rock. "Maybe...but what if I had said I'd take Danya? Not the timepiece? Tell me the truth now."

"Hef was going to shoot you. Either way, I score...but we're done now, right? Trade is a trade," Sky says with a slight chuckle.

Joe settles on the crest of the boulder, the fob-watch prominent.

"Yes, a trade is a trade," he tells Sky as he looks down the length of the canyon toward the shapes of people who mill like lost sheep.

Trader opens the dome's roof with the manual winch. He pauses in motion as he hears the front door of the church being tested.

"Nathaniel. Open this door. Nathaniel?" Sarah calls out.

Trader takes a deep breath. "Don't interfere, Sarah," he replies, his voice hollow in the structure.

Outside the Church, Sarah steps back, aims the shotgun and pulls the triggers to both barrels. The wood splinters as she rocks back from the recoil, almost losing her balance. Composing herself, she shoulders the door and charges into the dank, damp shadow inside the Church.

"Get out of here," Trader yells from within the dome.

Breathing heavily Sarah enters the study. She's cradling the shotgun. "Where is Danya, Nathaniel? I want her back."

"I don't have her."

The dome roof has opened and the sunlight dances off the suspended timepieces. Trader blocks the archway.

"I want my daughter back, Nathaniel. I made the wrong decision. I don't care about the diamonds or the blasted future."

"A trade is a trade, Sarah. Its law and laws are like Time. You can't change it."

Sarah points the shotgun at his stomach. "Will you listen to me you conniving sonofabitch -- I made the trade with you, not Sky. Now get her back for me."

"Are you going to shoot me?"

Sarah's bosom heaves as she lowers the gun. "I forgot about love," she whispers with the air of a deflating balloon. "That's not my fault, is it?"

Trader stares at her, unforgiving.

Danya stands adrift from the gathered crowd. Hef remains holding her by the arm, the barrel of his shotgun against her ribs. She senses a further disturbance amongst the villagers and when she looks, she sees the arrival of Mister Witherspoon and his flock. Their attire deeply contrasts that worn by the people of Erasmusville and, briefly, she thinks of clowns arriving in a circus...adding their colours, their made-up faces.

Danya steps forward and Hef pulls her back.

"I want to look. What harm can that do?"

"Relax -- somebody been getting between your thighs recently..."Hef replies.

"You pig," she tells him.

Reverend Dickinson stands alongside Mister Murray, aware of the new arrivals and feeling that he should be taking control. He can see Joe on the rock, and Sky hovering like a fly over a meal.

"Who would have believed it -- thought the man was honest, you know? Saw a bit of Erasmus in the fellow...a heart with a care," Mister Murray says.

Reverend Dickinson leans closer to Mister Murray. "Let's make certain no one goes any further into the canyon, Mister Murray," he whispers. "Trust me."

Mister Murray throws a curious look, but Reverend Dickinson silences him with a finger to his lips.

He has settled on the rock, the fob-watch in his hand. In the other he holds the strip of leather. The gathered villagers are becoming simple shapes to him as he begins to concentrate; he separates them from the real, places them as part of the scenery; even Danya. He must.

"What is the time?"He asks Sky.

"Three more minutes...can I come up there?"

"No."

Sky shrugs, swats at an insect. "Maybe I'll go down and see how Danya is doing. Join the crowd."

"Don't move," Joe warns him.

Sky ceases any movement. "What's happening?" He asks. He hears no response and looks up at Joe in time to see Joe bite down on the leather strip. Even from where Sky stands, he can see that he does not exist in Joe's world anymore, and this puts a flutter in his belly. "Shit," Sky whispers," it's hot."

He has one hand over it now and beginning to caress it. His sinew is beginning to respond, is tightening. A droplet of sweat is ignored, out in the open where the sun has no sympathy.

"I betrayed her love for me..." Sarah tells Trader.

"Life has betrayed us, woman. Youth has betrayed us. You betrayed no-one. We are the betrayed. We did what we did to survive," Trader tells her from the shadows.

There is sudden movement amongst the suspended timepieces and the sound of wind and dust against the windows and through the distant shattered door of the Church; a brewing, collecting sound, an army approaching.

"Nathaniel? What is happening?" Sarah asks, as she senses the sound, the change in the atmosphere, the pressure on her skull.

Trader watches his timepieces as they twist and turn under the baton of an unseen conductor.

"Not long, Sky. Not long," he tells the occupants of the dome shaped room.

The same gust of wind moves through the gathered villagers and tugs at Reverend Dickinson's cassock as if it were a hungry child. Villagers shrug deeper into their clothing, shrinking against the arrival of the gust and the sand it carries.

"Wind," Hef tells Danya. "Hate the wind."

Danya bolts. She runs for the canyon.

Joe sees only the face of the timepiece. It is his pivot. The sinew, the veins, of his hand have stalled, are frozen, responding to the electricity of his brain, its pulses.

The minute hand shifts ever so slightly; a shimmer of movement that is slight, but positive. It shifts in reverse, toward two minutes before the forty.

He ignores the insect with ruby wings that struts across his lips seeking moisture.

A stronger flurry of wind now blows and it disturbs the dead brush, irritating it into life.

Sky senses the change in the atmosphere and the flutter in his stomach becomes something more; becomes a niggling pain of doubt. His feet want him to move, but his brain reminds him of Joe's earlier warning. "Don't move."

Sky spins on his feet when he hears Danya's voice. She is calling for Joe. He can see her at the mouth of the canyon and she's is running; her lithe limbs sure on the terrain.

Sky makes a move forward.

His eyes are wide open but he is not really seeing anything anymore; shapes in a haze, someone running, just feeling and sensing, is being removed from this time, this moment as you know it, as you fly the thermal and look down onto the canyon below.

You see, as you glide, Sky teeter on his feet and then stand stock still as if he has collided with an object.

A shape of a man stands in front of Sky; it is translucent, a spectre.

You know this man from before The Event. He is a member of the Border Patrol, the sun darkening his sunglasses, the Glock pistol in its holster. He is walking toward Sky. He navigates the path between rocks, his riding boots leaving prints.

As the wind tugs your feathers, you witness Danya running past Reverend Dickinson. "Danya, stay away," you hear the Reverend shout as he breaks into a run after her.

Sarah Ferguson steps back from the vicinity of the dome as the chandelier of timepieces begins to rotate with increased velocity. Trader remains fixated as soldiers of dust pound the frail glass window.

"This is my time now, Sarah. He will be mine. My love, my heart..."

Sarah backs away, her fright sucking in her cheeks. She leaves the office and makes her way into the Church.

Aloft, you see the four Border Patrol members, the riders, in the canyon and they are moving cautiously toward the boulder on which Joe is seated. Their translucency peeks in intervals.

Danya, followed by Reverend Dickinson runs between the armed men. She suddenly hesitates, confused and frightened, her proximity to the spectres causing her to stop.

Sky does not move a muscle. He wants to. But he is petrified.

"I think it's about time now," a voice calls out; an unfamiliar voice to some, but not to you.

The villagers stand in silence as the incessant wind tries to obscure the events unfolding in the theatre of the canyon.

You are with Joe now as he senses the presence of the man beside him. Joe knows he cannot move a muscle, adjust a thought or even change the rhythm of his breath. He is in that space of time, and he captains it. The dials of the fob-watch work with him; are in tune with him.

David Erasmus squats beside Joe, chin on his knees, rocking in suffering, his throat tight and dry.

"What did you say, Mister Erasmus?" The leading rider calls out.

"What's he got in his hand?"

"I can't see. Can you?"

"Negative."

"Put it down, Mister Erasmus!"

Danya is spooked as these alien voices of the past reverberate around her. She is unaware of Reverend Dickinson as he closes in behind her.

You see David close his eyes and how freely his tears trail recent, salty paths.

"Put it down now!"A rider shouts; the rider that stands directly in front of Sky.

You see David Erasmus adjust the fob-watch in his hand, advancing its time.

Joe is a rock. The leather strip between his teeth does not budge, knuckles white as they clasp the fob-watch.

Time has married, has procreated history.

Inside the dome, the collection of timepieces, those souvenirs of the dead, are revolving with such intent, with such collected energy, a dull glow of white light begins to accumulate around them; a pulsating light as if being fed by a faltering generator.

In the street of Trader's village, Sarah is being buffeted by the harsh wind; it blows with strength and determination, lifting dust in its path and hurling the particles aside with anger. She keeps her head down but as she nears her horse and buggy, the horse panics and flees, the buggy bouncing comically behind the steed.

Defeated, Sarah struggles back toward the Church where the shattered door slams intermittingly like the rhythm of her heart.

From your height, you hear the threat in the rider's voice. "Put it down!" He again shouts, his words solid in the canyon, fighting the wind.

Sky sees the rider in front of him raise the pistol. It is pointed directly at him.

Joe is now aware that the man beside him has turned his head. He is aware that the man is smiling at him; that it is the smile a father offers a son after a term of absence.

"Hello Joseph," David says with a nervous smile. "I'm glad you came."

He must not shift. He must not react. The chain will separate; the links of time will separate. He must not flinch. But he knows that this is his father. He must not doubt it. No negativity but so many questions after so many years.

Sky sees the pistol in the man's hand jump. He feels the heat of the bullet as it passes his cheek; like the sting of a wasp.

The sound of the shot is loud. It snaps and crackles.

Danya screams. "Joe!"

She makes to run forward, but Reverend Dickinson, as weary and frail as he is, grabs her from behind. But she is strong; she is fuelled by her love for the man crouched on a distant boulder.

Do not shift even as he feels his father's body twist spasmodically beside him as the bullet enters muscle and flesh and exits cleanly.

Danya turns on Reverend Dickinson. She is about to break free of his grasp, but she is not prepared for the fist that he swings. It connects her on the jaw and he manages to grab her before she collapses onto the windswept earth. "Mister Murray! Help, please," Reverend Dickinson calls. He cradles her on his lap as he waits and watches.

"Of course it's me, Joseph," David tells his son.

"What's he saying? He's saying something?" The voice of a rider floats in the wind.

You see David Erasmus pick up the green, metallic box in his left hand. His injured shoulder hangs at an obscure angle. You see the wetness of his urine stained sock.

"Joseph - you must make it right," he tells his son. "The answer is in my mouth. I love you."

"Nathaniel," Sarah calls as she enters the room. She comes to an abrupt halt, a step away from the doorframe.

Trader stands in the centre of the lounge. His hands are by his sides as the tendrils of white light gradually engulf his frail frame; tendrils that writhe and grasp, slim and wispy...cocooning him.

"I'm finally going home, Sarah," Trader tells her.

Sarah screams and drops to the floor as a tendril of light snakes toward her, searches for her energy.

You see, from aloft, David Erasmus put his finger on the red-tipped rubber button on the metallic box.

Sky is fixated with the man in front of him; the man that is pointing the Glock. He can see his own reflection in the man's sunglasses. He can hear the foreign sound of static being broadcast over the walkie-talkie the man carries. He is aware that he in a place, a time, of no return, of recurrence.

You hear the air whisper between your wings as you hear the gun fire. You see the young man drop to his knees, his pale hands clawing at his heart before he drops to the ground.

You see the man on the boulder move. He lifts himself off the rock with whatever energy he has left in his drained body. He hurls himself to his right, toward the shape, the protection, of a coffin that rests on the ground like an uninvited landmark.

David Erasmus presses the button on the detonator.

It is not a blind leap he makes. In his hand he holds the fob-watch. He leaps from then into now; he carries with him the final nanosecond; that moment in time when destruction began, when the canyon floor erupted, fixed in a cog of time.

He soars to traverse the wall, to cross the gap. If he has left it too late, he will simply not remain.

Joe hits the dirt and keeps rolling and rolling, slamming himself into the heavy, wooden coffin left beside Erasmus's carcass. He struggles to reach for the lid...hands clawing for it...finding it...using it as a shield as...

There is total silence in the canyon. The gathered crowd hear no blast, feel no shockwave. In front of them the canyon floor is deserted of men, of the past, of Sky, of spectres.

It is as if nothing ever happened.

The bubble has burst.

My name is Dog.

I am a simple creature: I eat from a simple carcass. I ask for no more or less. I am good.

I fly your sky. From a height I witnessed the new beginning.

CHAPTER EIGHTEEN

In the coffin, all he can hear is the beat of his own heart. He is lying on his side, the lid of the casket still gripped in his hands. He has managed to close it as much as is bruised fingers allowed. An edge of sunlight intrudes. Is it today's sun, or the sun of the past that filters into the confined space? He does not know.

"Just Joe? It's me, where are you?"

Danya's voice filters through the wooden frame and he grunts as he pushes aside the coffin's lid. He rolls free into the dirt and comes to a rest on his back, the sun bright in his eyes. He closes them.

He feels her shadow. "You sleep in the strangest of places," she tells him.

"I wasn't asleep," he tells her, his eyes closed.

"No, I didn't think you were."

He sits up, every muscle in his body complaining. Even though she keeps her distance, she is close.

The villagers, most breathing heavily, have formed a semi-circle around him. Mister Murray and Reverend Dickinson are prominent.

"Is it done?" Reverend Dickinson asks finally.

She touches the bruise on her jaw as she watches him.

“I damn well hope so,” Mister Murray adds. “I’m not built for this.”

He stands. “Not yet,” he tells them.

A wave of nervousness ripples through the aged as they watch him make his way to the edge of the pit that contains the remains of David Erasmus, his father. He lies down on his stomach and leans into the pit.

“The answer is in my mouth,” he whispers to the skeleton. Delicately, he reaches into the mouth of the skull. His fingers roam across molar and incisor, canine...then they find the space, the indentation.

He hesitates.

“Thank you, father,” he whispers, as his fingers touch the coil of blueprint.

The town of Erasmusville has, by no means, become the Garden of Eden, but there is freshness to the street, to the houses and its inhabitants. Doors are painted, and a hint of greenery shows and wind pumps spin with reason and not routine.

A garden gnome fishes in a pond of water rather than a pool of dust.

Reverend Dickinson stands in the window of the house situated at the end of the street. He is clasping his Bible to his chest.

Through the window, he can see an active bee frolic over a blossom. The smile he wants to offer is quickly replaced by a grimace as the painful cry of a woman shatters the silence.

"Come on, come on...you have to push. I can see the head!"

Reverend Dickinson partly turns to look at the bed.

On which Danya lies.

Danya, her eyes closed, screams again and Reverend Dickinson fumbles with the Bible and glares out of the window into the street, where the knitting needles click furiously, the yarn either blue or pink.

He scans the faces of those gathered out there, those that are seated and knitting, those that await the news of a new life. He settles his look on Sarah Ferguson as she knits the blue yarn, her now opaque eyes settled on a distant vision as her hands work separately on creating a garment for the future.

The cry of a newborn child fills the room.

Joe stands near The Sow. He lights a cigarette and turns to look toward the horizon where the distant shape of the Monument holds its own stature.

"Joseph!"

Mister Murray's voice carries clearly across the plain and Joe turns to see the man hurrying toward him.

You begin to soar, to elevate.

Joe walks forward to meet Mister Murray, urgency to his steps. He flicks away his cigarette.

The spread of Kimberlite rock formations are vast and as you climb higher you see the movement of men as they work the alluvial dig, as they work toward a new beginning.

"You have a son, Joseph...a son!" Mister Murray's baritone voice tells the desolate land.

"How is Danya?"Joe asks.

" A-glow, Joseph. She is a-glow."

Now you are soaring higher and higher and as you look down you become aware that what you are seeing, is a part of your own country, wherever that might be.

It is barren, wasted, hot, but hopeful.

I am Dog. I am of your time. Respect it.

ABOUT THE AUTHOR

Mark was born in South Africa. He lived in Swaziland in the 1960's and returned there in the 70's. His unconventional life has led him to many parts of the world. He backpacked through Eastern Africa, the Middle East, Europe and Scandinavia (a period that was the basis of his first screenplay and directorial début) finally ending up in Washington D.C. working in the Australian Embassy. There he was smitten by the film bug and returned to South Africa where television production was in its heyday. Mark is now a recognised film director and lives in the United Kingdom. He is married, and has one daughter.

He is also the author of Two Feet, a novella about his unconventional upbringing as a youth in South Africa.

Cover design and artwork by Katie Roper

www.ingramcontent.com/pod-product-compliance
Lightning Source LLC
LaVergne TN
LVHW010041010425
807361LV00033B/250

* 9 7 8 1 4 8 2 6 3 9 0 1 8 *